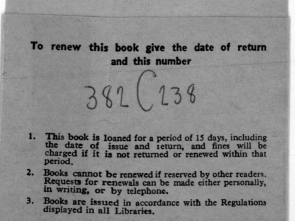

TODAY IS OURS

Julia decides to accept a job in Paris as personal secretary to Paul, a French business-tycoon. She finds him a strange man with unconventional ideas, who can see nothing odd in boarding his private secretary in his own apartment. He is difficult and bitter, trying to take revenge on Julia for the hurt his pride had received from his previous secretary. He had believed himself in love with her until she had run off with one of his business associates, and it was Julia who now had to suffer the brunt of his anger.

Fate, however has its own ideas on how our lives should run. How Julia succeeds in breaking down Paul's bitterness and how they find ultimate happiness together is shown in this charming romance by an ever-popular author.

BY THE SAME AUTHOR

Today is Ours

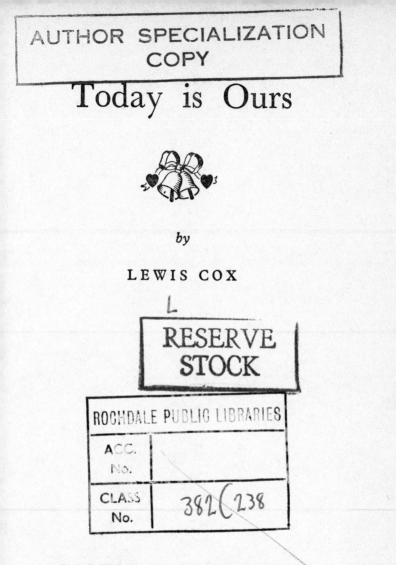

by

LEWIS COX

ROBERT HALE LIMITED
63 Old Brompton Road, London, S.W.7

PRINTED IN GREAT BRITAIN BY
BRISTOL TYPESETTING CO. LTD.
BARTON MANOR - ST. PHILIPS
BRISTOL 2

Chapter One

JULIA BROWN, fair, slim, pale, brown-eyed, walked purposefully up Bond Street. She paused at a certain door between two jewellers' shops. There were nine brass plates on the door jambs. One was printed "Ladies' Employment Bureau." Julia went in and up the narrow staircase to the top of the building where a black plate on the door bore in white printing, "Miss May Catchpole, Ladies' Employment Bureau." It savoured of Victorianism, but Miss Catchpole's name was almost a household word. "Please enter."

Julia went into a lobby with two doors, one marked "Private," and the other "Enquiries." Julia opened the door of the latter. A young girl looked up from a desk near the window.

" Oh, hello! " she said lightly, answering Julia's greeting, and popped a chocolate in her mouth. " I don't think there's anything for you yet—but go right in. You never know, do you?"

Julia's face fell, but she nodded and turned to another closed door within the room, knocked discreetly and waited to be invited in.

Miss Catchpole sat at a big flat desk facing the door. She was fair, fat and fiftyish, and looked at the newcomer over the top of her glasses which had slipped nearly to the tip of her nose.

" Good afternoon, Miss Catchpole."

" Good afternoon to you, Julia. Shut the door quietly please. My last caller went away in such a temper she has cracked the glass panel, and I am afraid it may fall out at any moment."

Julia turned her head to follow Miss Catchpole's significant look, and thought, Whoever it was went out in a fiendish temper.

Miss Catchpole watched her face in silence. "Yes, one hell of a temper! " she cried as though she read Julia's thoughts. " I hope you won't treat me to such a dramatic performance because I can't find you a dream job at once, or indeed, ever."

Julia half-smiled. " That means you have nothing to offer me," she said quietly accusing.

" You are not quite right. I have a job for someone, but whether it will suit you or not I cannot say. You girls all have one idea, the perfect job—short hours, big pay packets, little work, and oceans of adventure. Well, I dreamt of those things once, but they never materialised."

Julia really smiled this time, and May Catchpole caught the smile and found herself immediately in sympathy with Julia.

" What sort of a job is it, Miss Catchpole? I promise I won't be angry if it isn't exactly what I want."

" You must decide for yourself." Miss Catchpole sifted

the cards in her index box with experienced fingertips.
" Here it is." She selected a card and read, " ' Paul Roth,
Boulevard Haussmann, Paris. A business tycoon in property.' He wants an efficient and pretty secretary." She
looked at Julia. " Hark at the man! He's nearly as foolish
as you are. He wants the perfect girl, and you cry out for
a wonder boss. It just isn't possible to find either. Neither
dares even hope to get what he wants. The best thing to do
is to count the best points, and if either can answer a few
' musts ' satisfactorily, then it is wiser to come down to
brass tacks and either accept the job, or send the girl
away."

" Is he in London now?"

" Oh yes, at an hotel."

" Where?"

" The Hilton. Would you like me to follow it up for
you and make an appointment? Or do you think it is too
big a job for you? I have only spoken to Monsieur Roth
on the telephone, and though he did not say he wanted a
super-secretary, I gathered that that is what he wants."
She paused, her eyes on Julia's face.

Julia paused. She had been in and out of this office for
three weeks, turning down a few lesser jobs because she
wanted a big post with scope, something like this promised.
When she spoke it was breathlessly. " Too big! Nothing
is too big, Miss Catchpole. If you only knew how ' big ' my
thoughts are! "

" Don't tell me. I'd rather not even guess. Well?"

" Of course I'll apply for it."

" I hoped you would. It might turn out to be a ' snip.'
Have an interview. There is no obligation to accept on
either side, and sometimes when two people meet it gives
reality to a picture. I try to paint one for you which I think
is attractive, but I don't expect you to see anything through
my eyes."

She picked up the receiver from its rest and dialled Monsieur Roth's room at the Hilton Hotel.

While she waited to be put through Julia asked, "What is he like?"

"I told you I have never met him, *but* I have seen a photograph of him in the newspapers. He is dark, youngish and handsome—he could easily be some women's 'God's gift of a dream.' But his looks, with a hard mouth, may not be to your taste. You will probably, after my description, loathe him."

Julia thought, She's right, I shall. Aloud she said, "He sounds attractive."

Suddenly Miss Catchpole was talking to Paul Roth.

Julia sat down and opening her bag made up her face afresh. While pausing to look at the effect in her looking-glass, she could not help listening to what Miss Catchpole said, and it wasn't hard to catch what the man at the end of the line said.

Miss Catchpole spoke in that usual honeyed voice she reserved for clients. "I think I have the kind of secretary here that you require, Monsieur Roth."

She gave some essential details, then with a pained expression on her face she added, in answer to an abrupt question, "Of course I can't be sure. Most people agree that she is quite pleasant-looking. She badly wants a post in Paris . . . Ah, yes! I quite understand. The reference? No, there is no snag. It is only that Miss Brown has not had much experience. She has no former employer to whom I can refer . . . Who? Well, there is her cousin, Mr. Andrew Lester, the only son of *the* Andrew, who is willing to vouch for her integrity personally . . . I suggest you see her and form your own opinion. She is here in my office—now . . . What time? At once, within five minutes. She will take a taxi, and making allowance for traffic jams, she should be with you in fifteen minutes."

The man's voice was sharp and forbidding. Miss Catchpole nodded her head in confirmation of what he was saying. She bleated, "Yes, I do understand, Monsieur Roth." She replaced the receiver.

"What did you make of that?" she asked Julia weakly, an apologetic look on her face, and the treacle had gone from her voice and she sounded like a tired woman. "He's the kind of man who saps one's energy, if you know what I mean."

Julia replied composedly, "From what I could understand, I am expected to fly on a magic carpet to the Hilton."

"That's exactly what you should be doing. That man is quick—quicker than thought. He jumps to conclusions by instinct."

"And probably jumps to the wrong place."

"No, experience has taught him how and where to leap." Miss Catchpole meanwhile wrote Paul Roth's name on a card with her imprint on the top and handed it to Julia. "Try him," she advised. "Form your own opinions. He may not be so bad as he sounds. He is a bear and a brigand in one to me, but you may like him. Anyhow you can't afford to be choosey. Not many employers like taking on a girl for a responsible position without a reference. It is up to you to work for a good one when you want to move on and improve yourself. Indeed, you may stick there. One never knows."

Meanwhile Miss Catchpole had been watching Julia closely, thinking what a charming, fascinating girl she was. But never would Miss Catchpole dream of connecting such enchantment of looks with efficiency in business. They simply did not go together. She shrugged inwardly. That was not her concern. She had given Julia a chance, even if it was not a good one.

She added slowly, "Of course if you don't like him and feel you cannot work for him, then come back tomorrow and I'll put your name down afresh."

"I'll let you know either way tonight. I'll telephone your private address."

"All right. Now hurry, Julia. Take a taxi and tell the driver to hurry."

Julia ran downstairs and into the street, hailing a taxi

which happened to be passing at that moment. " The Hilton Hotel please, as quickly as you can," she said, getting into the cab.

Nothing happened to warn Paul Roth that Fate was preparing a pleasant surprise for him at the close of a tiring day's business during which he had been giving orders down Transatlantic telephones throughout the afternoon and his nerves were tense. Nothing led him to believe that he had reached a certain corner in his way of life, and was about to turn into a pleasant path, a kind of Eden, when things would never be quite the same again; or indeed that he might find a certain solace which would cause his nerves to relax and softer influences prevail.

Someone put a cup of scalding hot tea at his elbow on the desk. He drank thirstily, but his nerves were still tense when the empty cup was removed. The respite caused him to daydream—an unusual happening. He was hot and tired. It was after all the first day of Spring, and there was a warmth and quickness in the air which made him glance impatiently at his wristwatch, and wish that he had finished his business in England and was flying back to Paris. Not that one city was better than another in Spring, but his own car was in Paris, and he could get away quickly to his country cottage beyond the forest of Fontainebleau, where behind high walls he was shut away from all sight and sound of life. A swift-flowing river ran through the grounds. There were fish in it, lovely trout which, sometimes rising early, he caught in time to eat for his *déjeuner*. There was a luscious green lawn which he could lie upon, and cradling his head on his upraised arms, squint up at the blue sky overhead, relax and forget his worries. There were three Jersey cows in the meadow which provided him with milk and butter the whole year round.

The daydream ended abruptly when the intercom buzzer went and a message came through that a Miss Brown had arrived by appointment.

Paul stared into space. " But I don't know a Miss Brown."
Then his brow cleared and he said, " Oh, yes. Send her in."
He flipped off the intercom.

Before Julia could get there, Paul was already deep in
another telephone call.

He did not even glance at her, just waved a hand vaguely
in the direction of a seat, his mind full of the business in
hand.

Julia sat down quietly. In that first inquiring glance she
noted that Paul was young—his dark hair was short and
sleek, his shoulders were wide. She listened to the strangest
talk she had ever heard in her life. It made her smile.

When it was over and the receiver put back she was
still smiling.

" Miss Brown?"

Julia jumped. "Yes—sir." She stood and faced him
across the big flat-topped desk.

"What did you think of that last telephone call?"

She hesitated, then saw that he had not even looked at
her. He was looking for his memo pad on the desk.

" Go on," was the impatient invitation. He found the pad
and bent his head to study it.

" I—thought it most invigorating."

" Oh! " He hadn't expected that answer. Then he added,
" Is that why you had that grin on your face? I was going
to tell you to take it off. This room isn't a palace of fun. It is
a business office. Give me your card."

Julia fished in her bag, took out the card Miss Catchpole
had given her and handed it to Paul.

He read it, then looked straight at her, his eyes seeking
hers.

In the ensuing moments of silence slowly he put down
the card.

Then Paul spoke as a man in a dream. " She said you
were pleasant-looking, but I would never have called you
that," he told her. " It is a misleading epithet."

" I'm sorry." Julia's spirits fell. She had fallen short of

his requirements. Miss Catchpole had over-praised her and ruined her chances. She said quietly, " You mustn't judge me by my looks. I have had a thorough business training, and I am sure I can suit you very well if only you'll give me a trial."

Paul said, " Sit down. I don't question your qualifications, Miss Brown, though presently I will give you some dictation. You seem to have all that I want. But before I go further I should like to ask you a few pertinent questions which I hope you will feel able to answer. Why do you want to go to France?"

" I want to improve my French."

Paul spoke to her in his own language and Julia replied haltingly.

" You need practice," he commented, but his tone was noticeably softer. He asked, " Is that all?"

" No, I want to see the world, to have adventures."

" And do you think you will find adventure with me?" His tone was grim, even forbidding.

" I must begin somewhere."

" You are begging my question."

" It is difficult to answer."

" But you must."

" Then, no." She hesitated again and he said impatiently, " Can't you ever say yes or no without hesitating?"

For a moment Julia looked hard at him and it came to her how ruthless this man could be. Though his lips were sensitive there was a stony aloofness in his dark eyes. Stung by his impatience she cried, " Never with you, Monsieur."

" You are brutally frank."

" You asked me. I am sorry. I shouldn't have said that."

" Don't be for I did ask for it. I like to know where I stand. Please don't sit on the edge of your chair as though you have half a mind to bolt. I have not yet finished with you."

Julia sat back. Miss Catchpole had impressed it upon her

that this man was busy, yet he behaved as though time were of no importance to him. She was glad he spoke English so well because now all could be plain between them.

Paul said formally, " Thank you. I prefer that we shall understand each other clearly. You will stay in my apartment in Paris, so it would not be correct if we were friends. Your hours with me will be long. Sometimes I dictate late at night. You will not mind?" His tone said, " *You* cannot mind anything. It is for me to say."

She shook her head. " I can manage with little sleep," she ventured.

" Oh, I should not wish to rob you of your sleep. When we go to London you are free to stay where you please, but I do not often take you to London. The reason I want you in Paris is because my main work is done there; also it is important that you are English. My South American clients have a preference for English girls."

Julia did not follow him, but she said pointedly, " Miss Catchpole said you wanted a personal secretary." As if that explained her position, but of course it didn't. There was so much she longed to know but was afraid to ask.

" That means I may expect good service plus loyalty," he told her in a hard voice.

" My cousin, Andrew Lester, has told me something of the duties expected of me as a private secretary."

" Good, then I take it you understand what I want. Have you any boy-friends, Miss Brown?"

Julia shook her head. " None."

" Is that the truth?" he asked in surprise.

" Yes, why?" Her tone was not offensive, only inquiring.

" Chiefly because I cannot brook any interference from friends who think they have some claim on you. Also I find it hard to believe that you have no special boy-friends. With your looks you should have many." He was stating a fact, and appeared personally uninterested. A revolution of feeling swept over Julia as she realised that this man had not thought Miss Catchpole was over-complimentary to her, but underpraising her looks.

She flushed in sudden confusion under his quiet scrutiny, but managed to say calmly, " I have no close friends, Monsieur."

But he was obviously not satisfied with her answer. His eyes were fixed on her face as he inquired, still in that calm, emotionless voice, " Can you tell me anything about your background? I know already from Miss Catchpole's memo the basic facts, education and so forth, but I must know other things. It is important that I have a girl who has good morals yet is free from family criticism. I may ask you to do unorthodox things, and do not expect you to question why, but you must never slip up between right and wrong. Do you follow me? No one can afford scandal."

" Yes." Then she said, referring to the earlier part of his question, " I am an orphan. I have lived with my cousin's people for years. I have now a fourth share in a flat with some other girls, but we are overcrowded and they won't mind if I leave suddenly. I have no one who would question my behaviour. I suppose I rely on my own sense for that."

Paul liked her for saying that. But mostly he relied on the frank way her eyes met his, without that challenge and invitation in them which most girls had when he talked to them.

He said, " Could you entertain business friends for me if required?"

" I think so." She spoke guardedly.

" You can't speak with more certainty?"

" I do not know your standards."

" They are high. We must dine together and criticise each other. What about this evening? It is the only time I can arrange. I was leaving early for Paris, but I can postpone my journey for a few hours."

" I could, but I should like to know first whether you are going to engage me."

" Supposing I were not?"

" There would be no point in dining with you."

" It might be a stumbling block, but there are others. You would have to meet all sorts of clients, and yet be able to take care of yourself. You can't rely on me in any way. With your personality I am sure that won't be easy, though a girl with sound morals should not find that too difficult."

" Oh! " she replied and her voice was faint, wondering what on earth was coming next, sure now that what she had already feared was correct. The job in itself might be hard. It was the many sidelines that went with the job which were frightening her, for she was doubtful if she could cope with the clients he dealt with.

Paul was silent for a little while, contemplating her seriously. Then he said, " I propose giving you a month's trial, Miss Brown. I can promise that you will speak good French in that time for I rate you as highly intelligent. It is not a dull job and you will want all your wits about you. But the adventure you seek will have to wait a bit. The programme with me is work and yet more work. I am known to be a ' driver.' You see I am open with you. You enter my service with open eyes or not at all."

" And the pay? " she ventured to ask, hoping that he would appreciate her business acumen.

" Eighty pounds a month payable in francs, plus your board and lodging while working at my home, either in my apartment in Paris, or in my villa outside."

It was generous, or so it seemed. Perhaps though he expected extra hard work, something impossible. Being a business man, a ' driver ' as he was called, he would naturally expect good value for money spent.

She said nothing, only looked down because she did not want him to read her expression.

Paul asked harshly, " Aren't you satisfied? You should be. The last girl who was more experienced in every way than you, and suited me very well, had less. The man who followed her had more than you, but I could not work with him for long."

" Then why are you offering me more than the last girl?"

" Because I happen to want you for my secretary."

" Oh! Why did she leave?"

He paused before he said in a strained voice,

" I am not obliged to answer that, but the question is natural enough. She married."

" Oh! " Julia said again because she could think of nothing else to say.

" But if I keep you longer than a month, if I should wish you to stay, there would have to be an agreement with me that you do not marry for a year. That is fair enough. You are inexperienced. You will require some training. My time is valuable. You cannot expect me to waste precious time teaching you so that you may leave me to marry the first man who asks you. Or can you?"

Again she was conscious of a tense feeling about him.

" No." Then she asked, " When do I begin?"

To her astonishment Paul said in that tone which Julia had already recognised as brooking no criticism of his decisions, " Tonight, if your passport is in order and you can pack your clothes. You can return for a week-end later to settle any affairs you must leave over tonight. But don't forget that if you marry you leave my service. I shall have no further use for you."

Julia was about to protest, but she saw that he would not understand. A man of swift decisions it would not occur to him that those connected closely with his life could not think quickly, too. He was that kind of man, accustomed to giving orders and having them obeyed at once and without question. Like automatons, she thought. Something rebellious within her rose swiftly to meet his challenge, to beat him at his own game. If he could be quick she could be even quicker.

She said quietly, her face calm and her eyes steady, " I can be ready, Monsieur. But it is a step in the dark for me, for if you know little about me but what I choose to tell you, I, too, know nothing of you. I had not heard about you until Miss Catchpole gave me your name. But I am quite prepared to take the risk of going with you tonight."

A curious gleam came into his eyes.

" That is a good answer, Miss Brown. I am glad you have made your decision to go with me. I do not think you will regret it. You can trust *me* implicitly."

" Thank you, Monsieur."

He rose from his chair, a sign that the interview was over. He said,

" I shall make an early start. We can have dinner at the Airport before the flight. You must be there with your luggage at six o'clock."

She thought there was a shade of satisfaction in his even tone, but that may have been her fancy.

He went to open the door for her, and bade her *au revoir,* pleasantly enough.

Julia went out bewildered. The door was shut decisively upon her. The interview had passed as in a dream, and now it was over she had time to reflect that the last half-hour had taken on the aspect of a dream when nothing seemed real.

She pinched her wrist, and only when it hurt her was sure that she was awake. Julia would have been astonished if she could have seen how Paul Roth behaved after she had gone.

He had been surprised at his own reactions in meeting this lovely girl.

She'll be worth a cool million to me, he thought with immense self-satisfaction, and he enumerated many business associates who might be ready to grant him many concessions just for the sake of meeting this girl.

She's an asset, he thought with pride. Already he was moved by this pride of possession.

Plunging his hands in his jacket pockets he crossed over to the window and looked out. He noticed for the first time in months that the leaves growing on the trees outside were a tender fresh green. The intercom buzzed but he took no notice. The telephone bell rang. He was expecting a call from America. He did not hear it. A blackbird was singing among the branches, and he bent forward absorbed to see where it was perched.

Julia paused long enough before leaving the Hilton Hotel, to ring up Miss Catchpole. " I've got the job," she said tersely.

" Oh, I'm so glad. I thought it might appeal to you."

" I start for Paris at once, tonight."

" Well! You do surprise me. Can you possibly be ready?"

" I must. That's how everything always is with a man like Monsieur Roth. He works fast."

" I'll say he does! And what salary is he offering you?"

" Eighty pounds a month."

" It is far too much for a beginner. What is the snag?"

" That I've got to be ready to jump to it twenty-four hours of the day."

" Ridiculous! "

" Those are his terms. I dared not refuse."

" He didn't expect you to."

" Well, it was a take it or leave it attitude."

" I don't like it. In fact, I am tempted to tell you to refuse it, even at this late hour."

" It is no good. I've already accepted. I'll write to you from Paris and tell you how it works out."

" Do. I shall be waiting to hear. Why don't you get in touch with your cousin, Mr. Andrew Lester and ask his advice upon what he thinks about it all?"

" I will give him a ring, but I shall not ask his advice for I have no intention of taking anyone's." Julia's determination was a match for Paul's earlier expressed sentiments.

Presently, when Julia got through to Andrew and told him her news he was inclined to think that she had allowed herself to be rushed into something a stranger wanted. He quite agreed with Miss Catchpole's views, and was annoyed

and worried when he realised that for Julia there was no
going back on her words.

He said, " I had some news of my own tonight. I was
going to ring you up anyway. I go to Paris this week, too, on
an assignment for our firm. It is some comfort that I shall
be able to keep an eye on you. I'll drop in to see you one
day."

" You mustn't do that. Monsieur Roth is definitely set
against anyone calling on me."

Andrew exploded. " Heavens above, he can't expect you
to work all the twenty-four hours."

" There is no free time."

" Then he has bought you body and soul."

" Silly, of course not, but he is strict about certain rules
he makes."

" Why?"

" I don't know, but I promised to observe them. Of
course I didn't know then that you would be in Paris, or I
would have asked for an exception."

" Oh, all right, I won't, *but* if you have a few moments
to spare you must come and see me. Promise? Remember
my address, it is a small hotel near the Palais Royale.
Frankly, Julia, I don't like the idea of this job. You are
young and inexperienced. You know nothing of men, the
world, or business. I can't imagine why a hard-headed business tycoon wants a chit like you in his office. You're not
bad-looking, but there are thousands of girls far better-look-
ing than you, girls with ' it '."

" Then perhaps he wants somebody without ' it ' for a
change. I'm sorry you feel like this. You depress me. I was
so pleased to have landed such a plum job I thought you
would be, too. Even Miss Catchpole who put me on to the
job was mad because I had it."

" I don't wonder. It is all so odd."

" Do you mean he is mad?" she asked anxiously.

" Oh, lord no. *He* is all there, too much so. Most of
what you have told me is far too good to be true. You'll be

alone—with him—in Paris. You know, you want someone to look after you—"

Words failed Andrew, and Julia said, "Well, I've got to learn sometime to stand on my own feet. I'm not such a fool as you think. You must give me credit for having a little sense."

"It isn't only sense that you need. You are deliberately making yourself the victim of another's opportunity."

"I shall be all right. I promise you I will never get involved."

"I wonder. Granted you've got a clear head, I usually find that innocents like you do manage to get involved before they realise how things are shaped for them by others. However, as I am going myself I shall be there in case of need. What is your address?"

Julia paused in dismay, then she had to admit, "I don't know. I forgot to ask Monsieur Roth."

"Oh, Julia!"

"Well, I was hot and bothered when he gave me such a short time to get ready."

"So I should think. I never heard of such an unseemly rush to get a girl out of the country."

"It isn't a bit as you picture it. He was going anyway before Miss Catchpole arranged for me to interview him."

"Are you sure you understood what he required? He is French and your knowledge of the language isn't too good. You may have mistaken him." Andrew hoped it was so.

"Monsieur Roth speaks English perfectly. You'd never guess he was French unless he is deeply moved, when he lapses into French entirely."

There was a short silence, then Andrew asked suspiciously, "How do you know? Why should he be 'deeply moved' at an interview with a stranger?"

"I don't know why, Andrew," she said helplessly. "But I am sure that your fears for me are groundless. Monsieur Roth is a kind of robot. I only exist for him as an automaton. He seems hardly aware of me, except as a machine."

Andrew called that " Ridiculous. Damn funny business I call it. Look here, I'll be over in Paris on Monday, but if you want me before get someone to give me a call. It's no good pretending I'm not worried about you, I am."

" All right. I'll look for you on Monday. I didn't know you cared about me enough to worry."

" Well now you know you've got someone at the back of you, just see that Roth watches his step. If need be tell him I'll sock him on the jaw if he doesn't behave."

" You won't be called upon to do that," she said emphatically, then with a certain urgency in her voice, she went on, " I must fly. Time is getting short, and he doesn't like being kept waiting."

She was smiling as she put back the receiver. Dear Andrew, to be so worried about her.

Chapter Two

By THE time Julia had explained the new position to her flat-mates, there was little time left to pack. When she set out for the Airport in Cromwell Road, Julia had one large blue case only for luggage. Even then, she only arrived at the Airport by a late bus with one minute to spare before meeting Paul.

Carrying her own case she spotted Paul Roth at once. He was a man who stood out in a crowd though he appeared to take little notice of his fellow men. He was standing at the bookstall, an overcoat over his arm for the evening was warm. He was taller than he had seemed in his office.

Julia had time to look at him before he saw her. She thought he looked distinguished and debonair, certainly not the Bluebeard he had become in Andrew's mind. An official came up to him. They seemed to know each other. They confabbed together and consulted their watches. Paul looked vaguely about him. Julia guessed that he was seeing to her ticket, and there was some formalities to be observed before she could have it. So Julia, lugging her case, went forward to meet him. He saw her coming and moved instinctively towards her. Then he stopped suddenly and watched her approach. He raised his hat, then said abruptly, " Your passport, Miss Brown? I should have asked you for it in my office. It would have saved time."

" I didn't have it with me there, Monsieur Roth."

" You have it now though?"

" Oh, yes." Julia took it out of her bag and handed it to him. He did not look at it but gave it to the official at his elbow.

Julia said quickly, " You shouldn't have given him my passport."

" You will have it back presently."

" How do you know it is in order? You haven't even looked at it."

Paul paused in surprise. " Naturally I concluded it was in order." Then he asked curtly, " And your baggage?"

" Only this case, monsieur."

" Is this all?" he asked in surprise. He signed to the official to take charge of it.

" It is all I had time to pack."

" That means you will want to return for the rest next week."

She thought he was annoyed, and said placatingly, " I can manage quite well for a few weeks."

He dismissed what she said with a wave of the hand. " No matter, you can always buy more in Paris."

The remark made Julia want to giggle. Of course Paris was chock full of clothes, but they were not to be had for the asking. They must be bought, but out of what? Her salary was not due for a month, and nothing on earth would make her ask for an advance.

" You will find me in the restaurant," Paul told the official, and turning led the way to the dining-room. Julia followed in silence.

Paul appeared to be well-known here, for the maître d'hôtel met him with a smile, and the waiter hovered anxiously.

When they were seated Paul studied the menu, then consulted Julia. " I expect you are starving," he commented.

" I am rather," she admitted.

" Would you prefer thick or thin soup?" Then he asked if she would like chicken or steak, and gave the order to the waiter. He put down the menu saying, " We'll see how we get on."

The official returned then and handed Julia her passport. She looked at it carefully as though she suspected someone might have tampered with it.

" Is it all right?"

" Yes." Julia put it in her bag. Paul passed across her ticket. " You will notice that I have bought a return for you."

" Why?"

" Oh, you might feel like chucking everything suddenly, get homesick, or even take a dislike to Paris and wish to return to England."

" How can I feel homesick when I have no home?" she asked shortly, because for some unknown reason the word " home " brought an unaccustomed lump to her throat. " One place or another, it is much the same to me."

Paul did not reply, only looked at her hard for a moment.

Julia pretended to find interest in the scene about her. She had the feeling of an icy barrier between them, a wall that she could not penetrate. It made her ill at ease. She had no idea what to say to create even a pretence of friendliness with this man. What a fool she had been to take this post. There was no promise of lovely adventure, only continuous grind, and something within her rebelled at the thought of doing grinding work for this man. The feeling passed, and she found her tongue, saying politely, " I hope you did not have to wait long for me, Monsieur Roth?"

" Five minutes. As it happened *you* were on time. That is a good mark for you because I loathe unpunctual people around me. There are occasions when circumstances make *me* late, but you can have no excuse for being so."

Julia felt like retorting, You only deal with machines not people, but bit the words back in time, saying lamely instead, " I had much to do after I left the Hilton Hotel."

" What?"

She hadn't expected that. " I telephoned Miss Catchpole, and my cousin, Andrew Lester. Then I had to explain to my flat-mates that I was leaving them. It gave me no time to pack."

Paul listened indifferently, but he must have taken in what she said, for he remarked, " You could have passed over Miss Catchpole and written to her from Paris."

" I told her I would telephone the result of my interview before she left her office."

" Do you always keep your word?" he asked curiously.

" I try to." Julia looked down and knew she sounded smug.

" About this cousin, did you have to get in touch with him, too?"

" No, but Miss Catchpole was rather worried about me, and made me promise to ring Andrew. She is terribly efficient, but she is not keen on accepting responsibility for me."

" Why was she worried?"

" At my leaving so suddenly for Paris."

" How absurd! She knew that I was returning to Paris this evening."

" I know it is silly, but she didn't realise how—exacting you are."

" Thank you."

Hurriedly Julia went on, " I don't mean that in a nasty

sense. I was only trying to clarify Miss Catchpole's position."

"Don't bother. I shall not blame anyone. What about your cousin? Was it necessary for him to know your movements? When I inquired if you had any people who would worry about your movements you told me you had no one. Now I hear that this Mr. Andrew Lester is very deep in your life. Surely you do not expect to advise him of everywhere you go in the future? If so, you will certainly have no time for my work."

"No, only this first time. It was the last thing he expected to hear that I was going to Paris tonight. He was nearly as shocked as—" Here Julia pulled herself up and her voice tailed off.

"Go on," Paul urged impatiently.

"Oh, nothing, I was talking too much. It is not important."

"I insist."

"Nearly as shocked as I was to hear that *he* was going to Paris in a few days."

"To keep an eye on you?" The question had an ominous ring.

"All this was arranged days ago. He goes for our firm."

"Ours!" Paul's eyebrows had a questioning lift.

"The family company, ' Lester and Sons '."

Paul paused, his eyes distant with thought. "Ah, I've heard of them. They won't interfere with me."

"Oh, no," she cried. "It is the last thing they would dream of doing."

When they boarded the aircraft a queer sense of panic stole over her. Later, when Julia reviewed the happenings of the day she blamed Miss Catchpole and Andrew for her fears. At the moment, however, she felt too confused, her thoughts a muddle dominated by fear. It was as though a veil which had shrouded her senses all day, leaving her unaware of the sudden great change she was making in the

routine of her life, was rent aside. She had not fully understood the implications of this work she was embarking upon,
what it meant to her, and how it must appear to those who
knew. She saw herself as rather a silly girl, a puppet, who
was caught in a master's web, and the man who had so
cleverly spread it was Paul Roth.

Well, it was not too late.

Involuntarily Julia hesitated and half-turned to go down
the gangway steps, her slight figure poised for flight. A
woman coming close behind her frustrated this sudden
attempt to escape by giving her a sharp push. Almost without pause, automatically, Julia went forward into the plane.
She did not sit beside Paul Roth which was something of a
relief. He was shown to a seat in the rear of the plane.

When Julia turned her head to see where he was their
eyes met as strangers. There was no expression in his dark
eyes which returned her look with a blank stare, and oddly
it calmed her fears, and she wondered why she had panicked.
Gradually she quietened into a fatalistic mood and accepted
the position. Then they were all seated and belts fastened.
Presently the plane taxi-ed over to the far side of the Airport and there was another wait. By now the sky was dark-
ening to a lemon coloured twilight, and the Airport lights
looked like thousands of fairy lamps.

In place of her former panic Julia was aware of a wild
excitement which made her heart thump madly. This was
the moment she had longed for during her grown-up years,
to set out for the travels which had coloured her dreams.
Instead of being a monster Paul Roth was now a fairy god-
father, who was the means of making this dream a reality.
She was about to go forward.

A slight recurrence of that panic shook Julia when later
she stood with Paul Roth outside the door of his apartment
near the old Palais Royale. The passage was dimly lighted,
and in the half-light his face looked so strange and un-
familiar that the unnamed fear which she realised now had

been with her, well-hidden, throughout the journey to Paris, raised its head. For a short while she trembled violently, her nerves out of control, then with a superhuman force which pride called up to hide this from Paul Roth, she gritted her teeth and forced her nerves to some degree of steadiness. What helped her was that she noticed Monsieur Roth did not use a latchkey to open the glass-panelled door. He rang the bell, and waited impatiently, for he moved restlessly. Somehow Julia had not thought of any woman in his life— yet someone was in the flat, for the light inside was on, and a shadow moved about. She caught her breath sharply. Paul caught the faint hissing sound and stared down at her in surprise. There was no time for him to speak, for the door was flung hospitably open by a man in a short white jacket. He greeted Paul with a wide smile of welcome which included Julia. Nor did the man show any surprise at seeing her with his master. And Julia thought, perhaps Monsieur brings so many of his friends here. The surprise would be if he were alone.

Paul stood back for her to enter, and Gaston led the way into a salon, over-furnished in the French style with gilt on the furniture and dark crimson walls. The effect was warm and cosy, even voluptuous in the richness of carpet and curtains.

The manservant had bid his master a cheery good-evening, and Paul had replied, calling him Gaston. The name seemed to suit the small man whose head was no bigger than a turnip.

Gaston asked his master if he had had a pleasant journey, and did he need refreshment?

Paul glanced at the tray of drinks on the table—" Nothing more than what is there," he replied briefly. Then he added, " Show Mademoiselle Brown her room, Gaston. Let her meet your wife." There was a sardonic smile on his face which Julia did not care to see.

" Of a certainty, m'sieu'," answered Gaston, and turned to the door.

Pausing a moment in the hall to tell the porter to leave the baggage where he had just dumped it, Gaston led Julia down a narrow passage.

Passing a door Gaston remarked that it led to the kitchen. He scratched on the panel of a second door. "Our room," he told Julia. As he spoke his wife, an enormous round woman with a face like a full moon came out. She shook hands with Julia, made clucking noises of sympathy to Gaston, and said something about "*pauvre p'tite.*"

Julia's spirits soared. Everything was going to be all right. It was far more correct than she had expected. Miss Catchpole and Andrew could not find fault with the "set-up" in the flat.

Julia's room was small but prettily furnished, and she had a bathroom leading out of it. What more could any girl expect?

Gaston and his wife, Marie, were friendly disposed towards her, and Julia felt that here were allies in what she had already come to think of as her enemy's flat. She did not wait to unpack, but freshened herself up and presently, with some little trepidation now, retraced her steps to the salon. As she entered Monsieur was speaking on the telephone. Julia withdrew and as she did so heard him stop talking abruptly and replace the receiver with a click.

"Come in," he called out. "I have finished my call."

Paul invited her to have a drink, but timidly she refused, when he said abruptly, "Nonsense, I insist. It will do you good—give you courage."

"I do not need extra courage," she was stung to retort.

"Oh, yes you do. Otherwise why did you hesitate when entering the plane in London, and again outside this apartment?"

Julia flushed but said nothing. She had not known he had observed her panic.

Paul mixed a drink and handed it to her. "Drink this. It is strong but you need a booster."

Then he indicated a pile of correspondence, saying, "You

will clear these as soon as possible in the morning. Report here at ten o'clock. At eleven I shall want you to take some notes." He spoke casually, indicating what was expected of her.

Julia was glad of the lead and said, "Yes, monsieur." She drank some of her drink and found it potent. She felt emboldened to say, "If I drink all this I shall not know what you say or how I answer you."

"No matter, drink it. I take full responsibility for you," was the cold reply. He went over to a desk and opened some drawers in it. "You work here. This is your desk. You have all you want in these drawers. It is on the small side, but sufficient I think." He pointed to a covered type machine on a small sturdy table. "There is your typewriter."

Julia glanced about her, trying to take in all the things he pointed out for her needs.

Paul said, "If you want the desk moved nearer the window for more light, you can do so, only don't be distracted from work by the passing view."

Julia finished her drink. Her brain felt clouded. She went over to the window and looked out. "I should like to have the desk here," she remarked, "but as you suggest, it would certainly distract me from my work. The view down the street is enchanting." She returned to where Paul was standing by the table and put down her glass. "Thank you, I do feel better and bolder already."

"Then perhaps you will agree and notify those interested parties in the kind of man I am, that what you have gathered from the general lay-out of this apartment, and the sober chaperonage of Gaston and Marie, that I can be trusted? Your first instinct seems to have been correct. You took me at a fair value until they interfered."

"Yes, I trust you."

"I do not feel called upon to explain further, but believe me I have sound reasons for being indifferent towards you and all other girls. I shall never change, and so you can live here quietly and safely."

What could he mean? Obviously there were secrets in his
life which she did not know but which could throw light on
his curious and indifferent manner. Julia did not know why
but she felt depressed suddenly. There would be no fun in
working close to this attractive man knowing that he was
completely indifferent to you. Or perhaps she was depressed
by the effects of the strong mixture she had just drunk, for
suddenly the room seemed warm and close, and she longed
to beg him to throw open the window to the mellow spring
night, but dared not risk the refusal she knew he would
make. Besides she was standing too close to this disturbing
personality to feel complete mistress of herself. He looked
at her and through her as though he hardly knew she was
there.

She said, enunciating her words clearly, in case he mis-
understood her, " Thank you for speaking so frankly." She
giggled a little, why she did not know. " For what it is worth
I feel the same way about you. Between us we should get
through a vast amount of work. I like being busy, and I
hate being disturbed."

He looked at her sharply, aware that the drink he had
given her was strong, and that she was saying things which
ordinarily she would not say. " I'll keep you busy. There'll
be no letting up on my side. Even when I ask you to entertain for me at the end of a hard day's work, I don't expect
you to look a hag, but fresh and amusing."

Julia jibbed at the brutal manner in which he spoke. In
imagination she could see a whip in his hand, goading her
on to work harder and still harder not so much because he
despised her, but because he hated all women. But why?

She said, " I see. Is that all? If you don't mind I'll go
and unpack now. And if you don't need me any more tonight I will go to bed."

" No. I don't want you. Good night." The dismissal was
abrupt and hurtful.

As she shut the door of the salon Julia discovered that
her legs were trembling. They could hardly hold her up.

She stumbled across the little hall and down the passage to her bedroom. Someone had unpacked her case, turned down her bed and closed the windows. Noises outside did not penetrate and the room was quiet and stuffy. The bed looked inviting. Julia undressed and opened the window. She was glad to go to bed.

Chapter Three

In the morning Gaston in pin-stripe blue and white jean jacket, brought Julia's *petit-déjeuner* to her room. On the tray were blue jugs of hot coffee and milk and a warmed cup with three pieces of sugar in the saucer—a small napkin, a *croissant* and *brioche* and some pats of yellow butter.

Julia had never enjoyed a meal so much before. She would have liked to linger over it, but she remembered that she was no longer a lady of leisure but a working girl, with a high pile of correspondence to be opened and sorted out before Monsieur Roth made his appearance.

When she was dressed Julia went into the salon, and observed at once that the desk had been moved over by the open window where there was more light and air, and through which the sun streamed athwart the desk. In a mo-

B

ment of lightness of heart, Julia thought, I shall love working here. This room is so intimate and appealing. She glanced appreciatively around the room, then sat down at the desk and began opening the letters stacked on the 'in' tray. Most of the mail were business letters which she put aside for Monsieur to read and tell her how he wanted it dealt with. There were intimate letters from friends, mostly women, who wrote in extravagant endearing terms and seemed to know Paul Roth very well. Julia did not like the tone of what she read for they all assumed a personal right over him. Some letters were marked "personal" and these of course were unopened. There were many charitable appeals and begging letters. These were separated from the rest. Obviously a man of such importance in the business world would attract many demands on his purse. Probably he had his own pet charities. He would tell her. By the time he had been through this mass of writing she would know which to destroy and which must be answered—and how.

While she was busy Paul came into the room. He seemed calmer this morning, not so bitter. His tongue appeared to have lost its sting for he said cheerfully, "Good morning, Miss Brown. Did you sleep well? I see you have made appreciable progress with my mail."

"Thank you, monsieur. I slept well, with no dreams."

"Good!" He smiled because Julia was smiling. She looked young with that little round collar on her dress, and fresh because—well she was lovely anyway.

Paul came over to the desk, but before he could speak again, she said, "Thank you for having the desk moved. It couldn't be nicer for me. I will try not to let the view outside distract me from work."

He laughed shortly. "If I find you slacking I shall have it put back."

They discussed the letters. Some of those she had half-read because they were warm and personal, and evidently not for her eyes, Monsieur squashed in his fingers and threw them into the wastepaper basket with the remark, "Tripe.

When the basket is full, ring for Gaston to empty it." He ticked off various requests for charity. "There is a list in one of the drawers of those charities I subscribe to annually. Don't take on any new ones, but refuse politely. Now for business which after all is the reason for your being here."

His manner changed subtly. He became cold and aloof, determined and ruthless. He was a changed man. The telephone bell cut across all their talk. It never seemed to stop ringing. When Julia answered he listened to what she said. There were "notes to take," some intricate letters which he dictated to her, and which when she read them over to him, he changed completely. "You won't understand much at first, but that will come. If you must have explanations for clarity I would rather you asked me to explain than you should waste time in making mistakes." Paul hammered out an idea, expanding or contracting it, asking irritably for suggestions from her, expecting her to use terms and expressions that were both intricate and simple at the same time. All the while Julia was conscious that here was a master of his business willing to show her the workings of his mind, judging her to be of sufficient intelligence to understand what he was driving at. Sometimes when the flow of his talk faltered because he could not find the right word, she ventured to supply it, and to her amazement found that he used it in preference to a substitute of his own. Julia took many "notes" which would have to be typed during the afternoon. Each post brought letters from many parts of the world—

When a hooter from a steamer on the Seine went at twelve o'clock, Monsieur exclaimed and looked at his wristwatch. He seized the memo pad and saw that he was due to lunch with a business associate at twelve-fifteen. "Nearly time for *déjeuner*," he told her. "Better take a walk and come back at twelve-thirty, when Gaston will serve your *déjeuner*."

Julia's eyes were bright and her cheeks flushed. Suddenly

she was conscious of being tired. " Is it so late?" she asked. " I have enjoyed my morning."

"Enjoyed!" he repeated mystified. "Would you not rather have been out looking at the shops? Anyway, don't waste the sunshine. Get out now. In future you must rise earlier and take a walk before you settle down to the morning's work, or you'll quickly grow stale and we shall quarrel."

When Julia returned to the apartment Monsieur had gone out. It seemed strangely empty without his personality.

While she was out Gaston had opened the window and tidied the room. *Déjeuner* was waiting for her in a tiny room off the kitchen. She had grilled melon, a tournedos and some fresh fruit. Gaston wanted her to have a glass of red wine, but she refused. Afterwards she had some delicious hot coffee.

She went out again for a walk, meandering about the garden of the Palais Royale, not wanting to go too far in case there should be difficulty in getting back. Obviously whether he was there or not, and she worked alone, Monsieur would expect her to keep good office hours.

She began typing with a will. It kept her busy all the afternoon. At four o'clock Gaston brought her a cup of tea. " Like the Ingleesh drink." He made a wry face as she sipped it. Julia privately thought it " hot dishwash," but she could not tell Gaston that no Englishman would like it.

At seven o'clock, when it was twilight, Julia put on a hat and went to the post. It was a lovely lambent evening. Having posted the letters she strolled south until she came to the Seine, a smooth ribbon of steel in the early twilight. Crossing a white bridge to the opposite bank she saw the " stalls," black boxes, on the parapet above the river, containing old prints and books and other small articles. But the lids were closed and padlocked for the night, the vendors gone home.

Only one was open, lit by a couple of flares, an oasis of

light in the gathering darkness. Here was a man in a beret selling small birds in tiny cages. He offered one to Julia. She would have loved to buy a couple of tiny red cardinals, but she had nowhere to keep them. She would not have been allowed to keep them on the sill outside her bedroom window. In any case they were delicate tropical birds and would die if the weather were inclement. So she shook her head regretfully, and the man did not bother her any more.

She watched the river for a while, and looked across to the *Ile de France* to the twin squat towers of Notre Dame, and decided to explore that part of Paris on her first free afternoon.

It seemed years since she had left London, though this time yesterday she had not left it.

A feeling of intense loneliness that was like a physical pain came over her and she felt sick. Oddly, perhaps because he was the only person she knew in Paris, Julia thought of Paul Roth. She wondered if he had returned to the flat. She wondered, too, how he used his spare time, what he thought of her work, if he had already decided to keep her or dispense with her services at the end of a month. He was the kind of man to make quick decisions. Most important though, of all, had he missed her?

Of course not. It was easy to answer. She had been silly even to entertain such an idea for a second—so silly that she smiled at herself.

A passing Frenchman, caught by her good looks, took the smile as a personal sign of encouragement. After all, twilight was the hour of assignations for the amorous, when work was over and men relaxed. He retraced his steps to stand beside the " English mees," and examine her profile closer. He coughed to draw Julia's attention. She turned her head and he caught his breath. She was so fair and lovely and her eyes dark and tragic. He raised his hat, but she froze him with such a cold stare that he murmured an apology and fled.

Julia left the parapet, crossed the bridge and walked quickly back to the apartment.

Gaston met her in the hall, and told her in broken English and with some pantomime, that M'sieu' was entertaining friends in the salon. He had left a message that when she came in she was to join him there. "*Vite,* m'mselle," he urged, " or the people they will be gone."

Julia went quickly to her room, slipping off her hat on the way. She ran a comb through her hair, and powdered her face. She hurried to the salon and opening the door went in. The room appeared crowded with men. Her eyes sought Paul's, as though she were afraid of a scolding.

The men had been talking, but as she entered the room the talk stopped, and there was an expectant and surprised silence. They had been about to leave, but now they decided to remain, prepared to enjoy themselves. Paul introduced Julia as " Miss Brown, my new secretary," and was pleased with the impression she made on his friends. Obviously they envied him his acquisition. He poured out a drink for Julia. " It is not so strong as the one you had last night," he remarked affably. "You were out when I got back. Where did you go?"

The tone of his voice disarmed any resentment she might have felt for his curiosity. She thought, He is putting on an act for these people.

" Only down to the River. I had read about those ' stalls ' on the parapet of the left bank wall, and I wanted to see them. Unfortunately they were closed for the night except the one where they sell caged birds. I nearly fell for some cardinals, but alas, I have nowhere to put pets."

The other men had paused to listen. Indeed, they had not said much since Julia came in. Her light silvery voice was arresting. They basked in her smile. Without exception they suggested to Paul, " She must have some birds and keep them on her windowsill." But Paul demurred saying,

" It is forbidden by the terms of my lease to keep any

animals in the apartment. It is even a crime to feed the pigeons."

" But the windowsill?"

" It would not do at all. Besides cardinals are delicate birds and should be kept indoors. A late frost would certainly kill them."

" There will be no more frost. Soon it will be summer."

" When the sun will be hot and they will die with heat," Paul laughed. When they continued pressing him he said, " Definitely not in this apartment. Who would look after pets when Miss Brown goes away, and she will be going soon."

Now what did he mean by that? Anything or nothing? It was on the tip of Julia's tongue to suggest that Gaston could look after her birds, but that would be construed by Paul into taking advantage of his urbane mood. Besides, was he not putting on an act? He was never an urbane man. So she said with some finality, tempered with a mild regret, " Monsieur Roth is quite right. It would be cruel to keep birds here. But when I am really old and retire to my little cottage in the English countryside, I shall buy a talking parrot for company."

It took some time to explain this for Julia's French was not good, neither did Monsieur's friends speak English well, while Monsieur himself who could have interpreted for both sides seemed suddenly dumb on the subject. But there was a great deal of pantomime and laughter, a ready acceptance of mistakes by everyone, and Julia, under the influence of one cocktail was ready to laugh the most of all.

At long last the friends took their leave. Monsieur went with them to the door. They congratulated him fulsomely on his choice of a secretary. " How do you manage to pick such a lovely? Where did you find her?" *Ravissante*! and such-like expressive French words. They asked if they might arrange some pleasure for her in the evenings, adding, " She will soon fly away, having been bored stiff by an old sober-sides like you."

Paul refused with seeming regret, though Julia already
recognising some of the over and under tones in his voice
knew that he was boiling with rage. She understood enough
of the language to hear that she was not free to go out with
these men.

It's not fair, she thought rebelliously. Everyone is entitled
to some free time each day. It couldn't hurt him for me to
go with them. I should work much better if he didn't drive
me so hard and I could let up a little.

She heard Paul arranging to meet them next day for
déjeuner.

The door was shut and Paul cried crossly, " I thought
they would never go and meant to stay here all night." He
went into his bedroom on the other side of the salon. She
knew by the sound of his door clicking that he was vexed
about something.

It was a signal for her to go, too, and she went off to her
own room, passing Gaston who came into the salon to take
away the used glasses and tidy the room.

A short while later, her blood still seething rebelliously
in her veins, Gaston knocked on her door, saying that Monsieur wanted her at once.

Mentally bracing herself to meet Paul she returned to
the salon. Paul's back was to her as she entered the room
and said without preamble in a crisp voice, " Gaston said
you wanted to see me, Monsieur?"

He spun round to face her. " Yes, I want you to take an
urgent note. I will wait to sign it for it must go off tonight."
His voice was as cold as she had ever heard it, all the warmth
and bonhomie that had coloured it in front of his friends
was gone, and she thought drearily, I knew it was all a pretence. I should have known. She swallowed the disappointment and rebellion in her heart together with any softer
feelings she had for him, and tried to be businesslike. Opening a drawer in her desk she took out her pad and sat down,
her pencil poised to write, waiting for him to begin.

Paul seemed taken aback by her abrupt movements, but

he only said, "This is to Mr. Winter's firm. He was the youngest of those men who were with me just now—and the sharpest. Ready?"

"Yes, monsieur."

Paul dictated rapidly—even nervously, and Julia had to ask him to speak more slowly, for she could not keep up with him. He paused, apologised and began again. Warming to his subject he came over to stand by her, watching her pencil move across the leaf.

"That will do," he said at last, "etc., etc. Get it typed and I'll sign it. Anything to sign or report from this afternoon?"

Julia told him tersely. She handed him a pad which noted several telephone calls and how she had answered them, and what appointments she had arranged for him next day, and brought out a sheaf of typescript for him to read and sign.

"You've been busy," he remarked with some satisfaction, taking out his fountain pen. "I did not expect you to get through so much work, but I suppose it keeps you out of mischief."

He sat down, poured himself out a drink, lighted a cigarette and read through the letters, signing each sheet of paper.

"Well done!" he cried when he came to the last one. "I expect you play the piano well, Miss Brown."

"What makes you say that?"

"Because you've made no mistakes."

"I did, but when I read them over and counted my errors I did them again." She glanced ruefully at some crushed pieces of paper in the wastepaper basket, then waited for a "crack" about wasting paper. It did not come. She looked up at him, her eyes defiant and challenging, but he only said disarmingly, "It looks as though you want to hold down this job, doesn't it, hard though it may be?"

"I do. Andrew says I must get a reference for future use."

There was a pause and Paul said in a lofty voice, " Oh,
Andrew! "

Julia passed that by. He was in too good a mood for her
to take umbrage over his disdain. Obviously he did not think
much of Andrew's advice.

She bent to pull out a bottom drawer to get a new pad,
but the drawer was chock full and stuck. Paul had to wrench
it open. " What a mess! " he exclaimed when he saw the
contents. " Some day, when you have a spare moment you
might turn out this drawer. There is a lot of rubbish in it.
Throw the lot away."

Paul left early next morning for his main office which was
in a big building near the Bourse. Julia had heard of this
office and the forty clerks of both sexes who worked there.
Paul had stressed that she was on no account to mix with
them, that her work for him was strictly private, and not to
be discussed outside his apartment. She had replied, " That
won't be hard," yet it was hard already for working by herself all day without any companionship was tiring. But Paul
went there daily and had his *déjeuner* either in the canteen
in the basement of the large building, or at his Club. Sometimes, during the day, a Commissioner called at the apartment leaving tape-tied papers in a leather case which was
put by Gaston on the table in the salon, but Julia did not
touch them.

Andrew was delayed by illness from following on her
heels to Paris. It was nearly three weeks before he could
come. It seemed like three years to Julia. One day she
asked Paul if she might leave early in the evening to meet
her cousin.

" Your cousin! " he repeated vaguely. He had forgotten
all about Andrew Lester.

" Yes, Andrew Lester! "

" Oh, yes, of the firm of that name. Of course," then he
added, " Unless I may need you to ' take a note ' for me
when you might be a little late for your date."

" That is understood, monsieur."

Paul noticed that her spirits were brighter than usual. Her manner was excited and he frowned suddenly. How much did this cousin mean to her?

It happened that Paul did want Julia to take several notes. He apologised by saying, " Isn't that like life?" And he added, " Telephone your cousin that you will be half an hour late."

Julia kept Andrew waiting at the round marble-topped table outside the café in the Champs Elysées.

Andrew was drumming his fingers impatiently on the table when she arrived.

" At last! " he cried, jumping up and hurrying towards her. " I thought you were never coming."

They kissed each other warmly. She was so overjoyed to see him that her eyes filled with tears of emotion.

Andrew tucked her arm in his and they returned to the table. He ordered their drinks, and while waiting for them they took stock of each other. Julia thought he was thinner and there was a look of strain in his eyes.

Andrew asked many questions about Julia's life in Paris, but especially he wanted to know about Paul Roth, the kind of man he really was, not as rumour painted him.

She said, " I've had a dull time from a tourist's point of view. I've been too busy. Often, when work for the day is over, I have felt too tired to do anything but go to bed."

" You look thinner, Julia, and your nerves are tensed up."

" That's funny, I was thinking the same about you. Of course I'm tired. All this work is new to me, and Monsieur has a name for pushing people around."

" So I've heard." The drinks came, they toasted each other, then Julia went on where they had left off.

" He doesn't spare himself. He has many interests."

" Then he can't mind being busy. Why should he when he makes most of the cash?"

" I don't really know yet what else Monsieur does. So

far we've only dealt in property. He buys up old houses and builds blocks of flats on the sites which sell like hot cakes. He's the kind of man to have fingers in many people's pies —plum pies for choice," and she laughed at her small joke.

Andrew laughed, too, but bitterness crept into the remark that followed. "You bet they're plum pies. I can tell you one of his activities."

"What is it?"

"He's a kind of company doctor. He gets himself on the Board of a sick company, buys a large slice of shares when they are at rock bottom prices, then puts in capital, re-arranges policy and makes it well again."

"Oh!" And then she asked suddenly with a directness that discomfited Andrew: "Has our company had any dealing with him?" Fear had clutched at her heart. She would hate to let Monsieur in on their company. His methods seemed so ruthless. It would be a case of the surgeon's knife with vengeance.

Andrew paused and then he hesitated. "I don't know," he faltered, and instantly her heart buzzed with fresh alarm.

"Of course you do. Even I know that our shares have fallen rapidly and can't seem to rise, and I don't pretend to understand business."

But Andrew was not to be drawn. He gave evasive answers. Julia could not pin him down to the truth she knew he was hiding from her.

He said at last, "Be nice to your boss, Julia. I don't mean make a mat of yourself for his bad temper, but you never know when we may want his advice. He's known to be a keen bargainer and he could easily jockey us into the position of being bound to accept his stiff terms—a yes or no, swim or sink, with no hope of negotiating anything on our side."

She did not reply. She guessed now why Andrew had come to Paris. Her safety and welfare were the excuse. He wanted Monsieur's services, and he might need her help in coaxing better terms for the family.

" But you said just now——"

" I know." He spoke as impatiently as Monsieur. " It is an ' if '. It may not be easy always to get in touch with you at a moment's notice. If I telephoned and Roth answered he might think I put you up to things. He is sharp, and would easily suspect me of priming you. That of course would write ' finis ' to any business with him. We should need all his goodwill. I have heard that he was genial and human not so long ago, but that he has changed very much lately."

" I am always nice to him. Indeed, I have to swallow a lot of things I don't like just because he is the boss and I don't want to be fired—not yet, anyway. But he is naturally not nice to anyone."

" He's a bully."

" Oh, I wouldn't say that," she demurred. " Perhaps he is ill, and that is why he has changed."

" It isn't that. After you left London I tried to find out something about the real man behind all the hurly-burly of his big business. I heard a tit-bit of gossip that may interest you, and explain why he has changed."

" It is nothing to do with cash," she interrupted. " He spends liberally on making himself—and me, comfortable."

" This is personal and nothing to do with money. It may explain in part, too, why he is so hard on you. He is making you pay for someone else's ill-treatment of him. I understand that not long ago he was engaged to a beautiful girl. She was his secretary and they became engaged. Then without warning she went off with one of his friends and left his flat. She had been deceiving him all the time, living a double life, while he, poor sap, had believed in her."

Julia was shocked. She had not dreamt of anything like this. She said, " It must have been a terrible blow for him."

" I suppose so. Anyway he changed overnight from a decent sort of fellow to a brute with a vile temper and a bitter tongue. He swore he would never trust another woman again. He is one of those men who take amorous rebuffs hardly."

Julia was silent. She contemplated her half-empty glass. She was conscious of a sense of loss. Even to herself Julia could not put into words what she had hoped for from Paul Roth. But whatever it was, such hopes of friendship that she did have and perhaps subconsciously counted upon were doomed from the beginning. The other girl had not only ruined Monsieur's life, she had damned the future for any others who came after her. So many small incidents were now made plain to Julia. Paul's indifference to her own charms, and she had tried to charm and please, his boredom when she spoke to him outside business matters, his unaccountable irritation over small mistakes. He had no patience. He never exerted himself to be pleasant. He drove others because he also was the victim of that insane drive, and as he could not stop himself so he would not let others pause.

She toyed with the idea of trying to find a weak spot in the armour he had put around himself, determined never to be soft again or permit anyone to penetrate that armour. In her wretchedness of mind Julia forgot about the Lester Company which was doing so badly in England. She did not even notice that Andrew's manner was unnatural, and that he was obsessed about his company, that without telling her too much he was trying to win her sympathy and perhaps, her help.

Andrew touched her hand which was resting on the marble table, and she came back to the present with a start. "You are not drinking your sirop. Don't you like it? It seems a mawkish drink to me. Why not leave it and try something stronger? You need bucking up. All your gaiety has gone. Or perhaps you are hungry! What about going to some other place and getting a hot supper?"

"No, thanks. I'm not hungry. It is getting late."

Andrew glanced at his wristwatch. "What time have you to be in?"

"I have no idea. I suppose I can stay out as long as I like. I have a latchkey, but if no one tells Gaston I am out he may bolt the door and go off to bed. He was out when I left the apartment or I would have told him not to lock up."

" I don't want to have a row with your boss through keeping you out too late."

" Don't worry. I can manage him."

" Can you, Julia? Can you?" he repeated pathetically.

She replied sturdily, but in her heart she was not so sure.

" When do you go back to London?" she asked.

" Not yet. And you? I understood you were coming over to get your clothes."

" Yes, I must go soon. I have only two dresses with me, and Monsieur will soon get sick of seeing me in the same old clothes. He is rude enough to remark on it, too."

" It's like that, is it? But his rudeness is a guard that I like. He is hardly likely to attempt any love-making while he is so rude. The two don't go well together."

She flushed. " He doesn't connect me with love and passion. We have never ' clicked '," she confessed, and felt that she had failed somewhere as a woman.

" It's just as well. While I am here we can meet every evening and explore Paris. I couldn't take you around like he does because I haven't the cash to spill that he has—"

" Don't worry," she broke in. " Monsieur does not like my company sufficiently to ask me anywhere. Being in the flat so long at a stretch is like being in prison. Gaston and Marie like me and would do much for me, but they can't interfere with the work, which comes first, and is of course the reason I am there."

Andrew seemed resentful. " That man makes a slave of you."

" Only because he happens to be that kind of man, and as you say, has suffered cruelly at the hands of a lovely girl. After all he has engaged me and is trying to show me his ways. If I am too dumb to learn I can't blame him for getting furious with me. He is a busy man, yet finds time to show me many things I could never know, if left to myself."

" I bet he expects to make, even out of you. Have you ever

asked yourself, Julia, *why* he does it?" Andrew asked in perplexity.

" I know. He is a perfectionist. He took me, raw material, because he thought there was something in me which would repay him for any trouble he took over me. While there is room for improvement in my work and I show some results for his teaching, he will continue doing it—"

" You say you've learnt a lot."

She laughed lightly. " Oh, so much. Talk about a shipboard acquaintanceship—I am cooped up in that small flat with him—at least, he is often out, but the personality remains. Sometimes I feel stifled, it is so overpowering. When I leave him I shall be fully trained and experienced and ready to take on a bigger job with lots of scope and initiative. I want to work hard now, for my own future."

She laughed as she spoke of her future position in the business world, but her heart was like lead, for what was the use of working for an attractive man whose heart was emotionally dead?

" You may marry long before such training will be of much use," Andrew hazarded.

" Someday, but not yet. I've got to repay him before I dream of doing that. Anyway, I'm not the sort to walk out on him like his former secretary."

" Perhaps he knows that?"

" Perhaps that was why he chose me—a kind of Martha."

Chapter Four

THE EVENING soon passed and Julia talked herself into a
better mood. When Andrew took her back to Paul's
apartment at midnight he said, as they parted outside the
door,

"Even Roth can't grumble at this hour."

He tried her key in the door but could not get in.

"Gaston must have thought I was in bed and locked the
door," she whispered. "We'll have to ring the bell. It is
later than I expected to be out. Perhaps everyone is asleep,"
and she giggled at this predicament.

"Tell him you have been with me."

"It wouldn't cut any ice because he knows. He won't

mind unless some unexpected business has cropped up, and he wanted me to ' take a note '."

She laughed again, a pretty tinkling sound. " I remember reading once that Mary, Queen of Scots said if they could see her heart after she died they would find ' Calais ' written on it. I know what would be written on mine." She mimicked Paul, saying in a deep voice, " ' Take a note.' If I've heard those words once since I came to this apartment, I've heard it a hundred times."

She finished laughing on a light note, because to compare herself with the illustrious Mary, Queen of Scots was ludicrous. Also being locked out made her feel reckless, like throwing her bonnet over a windmill, and having to ask Monsieur for a new bonnet. She did not understand that Andrew was looking desperately at her, mouthing to her to " shut up." She only saw the quick grimace on his face, and that struck her as funny, too.

Something made her understand! She turned swiftly to the door. It was open and Monsieur was standing on the threshold. He must have heard what she said. How much had he heard? The laughter died from Julia's face. Inane remarks that had seemed so funny a few seconds ago when she attempted to imitate Monsieur were funny no longer. She was confused and abashed. Of course she should have been more careful. What a fool she was. Picked out of their context those words made it look as though she were disloyal to Monsieur. Julia wished she had not been so frank with Andrew, or said anything personal to upset Monsieur's humour. With a scarlet face she said " Good night, Andrew," over her shoulder and walked past Monsieur into the apartment, feeling very small indeed.

As the door shut behind her she said, " Thank you, Monsieur, I am sorry to disturb you. Gaston was out when I left earlier, or I would have told him not to lock up."

" You could have put a note on the table here."

" I didn't think to do that. I am sorry. Good night." She paused uncertainly. " Do you want any business done?"

she asked. She dared not mention those fatal words, "Take a note."

"At this hour!" he smiled sardonically.

"I don't mind."

"Would you like a drink?"

"No, thank you."

"Hungry?"

"Not a bit."

"I should not like anyone in my home to go to bed hungry."

How cold his voice was.

"Gaston gave me a good dinner before I went out."

"That was some hours ago. I should have thought your cousin—it was your cousin?" Julia nodded briefly, "would have given you supper."

"Andrew offered to take me to one of those all night places, but I preferred to return here."

That remark seemed to put him in a good temper, for his tone was warmer as he said, "You showed good sense. There is no point in trying to work and play for twenty-four hours on end."

If Monsieur had taken that tone with her last night she would have rebelled, but in the light of what Andrew had told her of his blighted love life she was too full of pity for this man to mind his coldness. Meekly because there was nothing useful she could say to him to mend his broken heart, Julia said "good night," and went to bed.

Next morning was one of those glorious days when the air is fresh, the sun warm and the skies blue. Having had her *petit déjeuner* in her bedroom beside the open window Julia went into the salon and sorted the mail which was lighter than usual. Then she went for a short walk. The shops were open and she bought herself some pink ribbon and returned to work for an hour. Then she wanted some advice.

While waiting for Monsieur to appear at eleven o'clock,

she opened wide the big window of the salon, and sitting on the window-ledge, one foot just reaching the ground, and the other idly sawing the air, she enjoyed the golden sunshine. She even hummed a song a Greek minstrel had sung at their café table last night. She was not so much happy as lighthearted by the morning glory.

Perhaps Monsieur, too, had felt the call of the morning freshness and promise, for he came unexpectedly into the salon half an hour earlier than usual. He appeared as surprised to see Julia as she was to see him.

Hurriedly she jumped to her feet on the thick carpet and slid the window down, recalling guiltily that Gaston had once explained to her that the furnishings in the room were costly, and open windows let in dirt and sunshine which would cause them to soon perish.

" Don't move, Miss Brown." She stopped astonished. " You were enjoying the air. What was that song you were humming? I do not know it. It has a gay lilt."

" It was only something I heard on the boulevard last night. I caught two lines of it."

She spoke soberly and Monsieur noticed that the radiant look on her face had faded with his coming. He said, " Open the window again and sit on the sill, not that it can possibly be comfortable. Put a cushion under you."

" I would rather get down to work now that you are here. There is a letter I do not understand—"

" Let it wait. I prefer not to work until eleven. Besides, I have something to say to you."

Julia's face went white. It's a lecture about last night, she thought with dismay. I thought his letting me go off to bed so easily was too good to be true. He's upset by my silly remark to Andrew and is going to preach loyalty or something like that. But she obeyed him by opening the window again and trying to assume her careless attitude on the sill. She did not use the cushion and it was very uncomfortable.

Monsieur came to stand beside her.

" It's about your clothes," he said abruptly, not looking at her.

" Clothes! " she exclaimed blankly, her eyes wide with astonishment, on his face.

He did not look at her, but said, " Yes, clothes. I have tried to improve your business knowledge. I have arranged for you to begin French lessons, tomorrow evening. Your accent is atrocious and your vocabulary poor. But that isn't all. There are other things you must learn, what every woman is supposed to know here—how to dress."

Oh! thought Julia, who had believed her French was fair. She needed practice, of course, but she could understand this language better than she could speak it. Trying to talk made her shy. But clothes were another matter. It was cheek of him to criticise her clothes!

Paul went on talking. He said, " You have been here several weeks, and during that time I have seen you in two dresses only."

Julia hung her head. He's sick of the sight of them, she thought, and recalled the bother of having to wash muslin collars every night and borrow Marie's iron each morning, trying to make the best of her wardrobe.

She said coldly, because it was presumptuous of this man to talk to her about clothes, " I'm sorry if you don't like them, monsieur. When I have a few moments to spare I must go to London and fetch all my clothes. It must be done soon."

He was silent and then he said oddly, even whimsically, " You may find that you prefer London to Paris, and change your mind about returning."

" I like Paris," she told him stubbornly.

" Also, those dresses would not be French."

" No, but I have several nice English dresses off the peg."

Paul nodded as though he understood but it was clear that he had never heard of the expression, " off the peg," for he said, " No doubt they are nice but hardly *chic*. I prefer

French clothes. Why not take time off after *déjeuner* and buy some new dresses in Paris?"

Julia shook her head. "They would cost too much. Besides, I have no money yet for new clothes. Though I haven't a rag fit to wear I must manage with what I have until the end of the month."

"That may be practical, but it is not desirable from my point of view. You must draw your salary in advance, and pay *back* from next month's as you can."

Julia objected. "That would be tying a millstone around my neck at the outset of my career. I'd rather wait if you don't mind."

She did not like discussing clothes with him. She did not care to think that he must have looked closely at her dress, probably making a mental cost of it, and disparaging it. She was chagrined that he thought so little of her dress, and felt that he should have kept his opinion to himself.

"But I mind," he said heatedly, sensing her obstinacy to fall in with his wishes.

"Then do not look at me," was the sullen reply.

"I try not to, because it gives me, how you say it, a pain in the neck."

He was confusing English and French. She knew the sign, that he was getting heated. "Well, if you do not wish for an advance on your salary, I suggest you apply to the treasurer at the main office of the company for the cost of a couple of outfits suitable to wear at the races. Remember I do not care to be seen there escorting a badly-dressed girl. I would be a laughing stock to my friends."

As if I care, Julia thought, but her spirits rose when Paul spoke of going to the races. But he disdained her company because of her poor wardrobe. She said frankly, because she was so deeply moved by this personal talk, "I am sorry, Monsieur, not to be able to go to the races with you. I should hate to be the cause of laughter among your friends. Personally, as I am situated, I should prefer to stay here and work."

" Rubbish! You are, or should be, an asset to me. Do you not realise that I do not wish for the pleasure of your company for myself, but because your presence in my party will help to balance it? I know few girls of your age."

Julia replied stubbornly, " I can only repeat what I have already said. The races are out for me."

" Hoho! You rebel! Well, we will see. The matter is now dropped for a while." He relapsed into his own language speaking dramatically for a few moments, and Julia could not follow him. She only knew that he was now angry and excited, and so French came to his tongue more easily than English. He said, too, " I had in mind a visit to the races today. It will be delightful at Longchamps. But you cannot go. Your clothes would disgrace me."

Julia went white with anger. She rose to her feet. She was shaking with rage and humiliation. She said in a low tone, which made itself felt far more than angry words would have done, " I will leave you now."

She turned to flounce out of the room, but he caught her arm in a steely grip—" It is absurd that you insist on being obtuse. Part of your contract with me is to accompany me when I do business. The races are an excuse to do business in pleasant surroundings, just as I take an expensive box at Ascot in June and invite my business friends to join me there. A male party would be boring, We must have pretty girls. To appear in those places you've got to dress well." And he thought, I do not mind what you wear or how you wear it. It is the person inside the dress that counts. But he did not say this. He saw that she was really roused and was ready to hurl words at him like stones, words that she would soon regret saying, and that he as boss, dared not overlook. He let go her arm. He passed his hand wearily across his brow.

" All right, go. You've spoilt this lovely morning. Don't bother to work. In your present mood it could not be good."

Almost before the words were said, Julia had gone from the room.

Gaston came into the salon. He looked furtive and hostile, and Paul shouted to him to get out. He lighted a cigarette, and stood by the open window, puffing violently and not finding any pleasure or consolation in the cigarette.

Five minutes later Marie came in. Paul could not shout to her to clear out. She was a woman and her face was calm and smiling as usual. She had no quarrel with him. Also she was one of the best cooks in Paris and he did not want to lose her. He said lamely, " Mademoiselle has gone to her room."

" I know, m'sieu'. I believe from the opening and shutting of drawers that she is packing her case to go to London." She spoke gloomily and Paul was startled.

" Oh, surely not?" he cried in a shocked tone as the words sank in. He recovered quickly for Marie was looking at him with wide-open eyes, an almost too-innocent look. He said, " But I am not surprised. She hates me so."

" Did she say that, m'sieu'?" It was Marie's turn to look astonished.

" No, but she acted it."

" And all about clothes, was it not, m'sieu'?"

" Yes, I wished that she should buy a dress suitable to wear at the races, and she refused. It is as silly as that."

" Clothes cost money, and she cannot afford them."

" I have pointed out several ways of getting dresses."

" Which are not acceptable to M'm'selle. *Tiens*, M'sieu'! " Marie became conspiratorial. " I may be able to help. My cousin's daughter, who is a machinist at one of the big houses will be willing at a low cost to run up some dresses for her. I shall see her this afternoon. Perhaps M'm'selle can be persuaded to give an order."

Paul was delighted with Marie's practical offer of help, for his own efforts with Julia had reached an *impasse*. He said quickly, " Send Mademoiselle to me and I will pass on your suggestion. Whatever happens we must stop this mad idea of her going to London in such a mood. She would never return. *Vite*, Marie, *vite*! "

A short while later Julia, looking chastened, and a little frightened now, came into the salon. " You wanted me, monsieur?" she asked colourlessly.

Paul had no idea that she was fighting for composure, sure that any display of emotion would swiftly put him in a worse rage with her.

" I had to see you, Miss Brown," he replied somewhat simply.

" To give me the sack?" she asked, looking down.

" Why, no! *Bon dieu,* where did such a silly thought come from?"

" I was rude to you, monsieur."

" Perhaps I asked for it. I should have approached you more tactfully. I hurt your feelings and naturally you were annoyed."

" Then why did you send for me?" she demanded suspiciously.

" To tell you that Marie has a cousin who copies model dresses, and she is going to ask her to make some for you."

Julia brightened, then her face clouded again. " She will charge the earth. I know what these little dressmakers are. I can't afford much."

" Well contact her first and find out before you despair."

" Then you don't want me to go back to London?"

" Certainly not. Your going now would mean an admission of failure on my part. I do not believe you are one, or ever will be."

" I was so sure you would send me away I began to pack."

" I thought you were so angry with me you had made up your mind to go."

They looked at each other. Suddenly Paul smiled broadly. Julia looked so young and woebegone, so much at his mercy, that he had to smile to comfort her.

The smile was so unexpected and infectious that Julia

grinned back at him. Simultaneously they burst out laughing.

This break in the tense emotions that were mounting between them had to come, even though afterwards things settled down quickly to what they were before. Often Julia, reviewing that morning in retrospect, wondered how or why they had broken down, even for those few minutes, that barrier which had always been between them from the beginning.

Paul was soon himself again, hard, driving and unsympathetic.

There were days when Julia recognised from a certain timbre in his voice that he was unapproachable, and it was wise to keep out of his way, for she came to fear the lash of his bitter tongue though in her position she could do nothing to stop it. Nothing she did seemed to please.

Sometimes business acquaintances came to the apartment for drinks, and she was expected to join them. She did not mind now for Marie's cousin had been a great find. She made several dresses for Julia at reasonable cost, and these she delighted in wearing, especially as Marie's cousin had given her hints on the right accessories. There had been two pay days and Julia spent all the money she could on clothes and cosmetics, anything which would place her above Paul's criticism.

Though Paul never spoke to her again of clothes he must have remarked on the change in his erstwhile mouselike secretary. His friends were enchanted with her, and never stopped singing her praises. Indeed, one man, braving Paul's displeasure by taking too much notice of this prize possession, actually had the temerity to send Julia gifts of flowers. He invited her to dinner and the theatre because he longed to improve on her acquaintance away from Paul.

Julia refused the dinners because Monsieur invariably asked her to " take a note " in the early evening. Sometimes she suspected that he arranged to do this for the sole purpose of preventing her going out, and no doubt had she inquired he would have found a certain satisfaction in saying this was so. But Julia did not question. She was always agreeable to falling in with his wishes no matter how awkward his timing. But she could not prevent this South American from sending her glorious flowers done up in cellophane paper. Anyway, she did not want to, for she loved flowers.

One morning a florist's girl arrived at the apartment with a lovely sheaf of dark red roses. They were delivered before Paul was up though usually they came later and he never saw them. So glowing and gorgeous was the gift that when Julia unwrapped it she selected half a dozen which she arranged in a vase and put on her desk in the salon.

Of course Paul came in at a wrong moment and spotted them at once. For a long second Julia thought he was going to say, " What lovely roses! " Instead he demanded in a sharp staccato voice, " Who sent those flowers? "

Julia knew at once she had made a mistake. She replied truthfully, " The card said they were from Señor Don Felipe Monti."

Paul's lips were compressed. " What impertinence! When did they come? "

" Just now. They are so lovely I thought you might like some."

" Share another man's roses! What do you take me for? You know I hate flowers in an office. Take them away."

Her face clouded. She might have known how it would be. She reached for the vase, and he saw her bend over the flowers and smell their subtle perfume appreciatively.

What possessed him to act as he did Paul never knew. Before she could lift the vase off the desk he had leant across, seized the flowers from the vase and thrown them into the wastepaper basket. " That's what I think of the señor's roses," he cried.

Julia's face darkened with anger. " How dare you throw away my flowers," she cried and stooped to pick the bruised blossoms from the basket.

" They were not yours. You gave them to me, and I don't want them. You know my views on the distraction of flowers in an office. What is the use of telling you if you take no notice of what I say?"

" I forgot. I only wanted to share something nice with you."

" *Dieu*! The señor meant them for your enjoyment not mine," he snapped.

" It was a pity you had to vent your anger on the flowers, monsieur."

He gave her a long look, and a queer expression flashed across his face and was gone. He passed his hand across his brow as though he would dispel some worry which had gathered there, then without another word he walked out of the room.

" I don't know why I put up with him in these rages," she cried aloud wrathfully.

She did not see him until the following morning, when he appeared to have forgotten the episode. Anyway, there were no flowers in the room to remind him.

But Julia observed that the señor was never asked to the apartment again. Paul gave her more work to do than ever. She had French lessons every evening, and her teacher praised her to Paul.

When he mentioned the praise to Julia, he said, " When you have mastered French, you may wish to take up another language."

" I am content with one," said Julia quickly, and longed to have a little time to herself.

" Don't be lazy, Miss Brown. Now is the time to learn while you are young and can assimilate easily."

She stuck out her chin in what was meant to be an aggressive pose, which privately Paul thought funny. " I don't think even my worst enemy could call me lazy, monsieur, even you who are blind to any good points I may have."

" I am not your enemy. I am your friend," he remarked

blandly. "And as I am not blind I see all of your good points."

Julia did not reply. She thought, you have a funny way of showing your friendship. But solely to please him, to be able to follow that spate of French sentences he hurled at her when in a temper, and which up to date she could not understand, Julia redoubled her efforts with French.

"Madame Sueret says she will take me to the Comédie Française one evening," she told Paul in an expansive moment. "She looks upon it as part of my language education."

"Now why didn't I think of that? *Bien*, we will make a party of it," was his cheerful reply.

That wasn't Julia's idea at all. She did not mention going to the theatre again. If Paul came he might be in one of his moods and so spoil her fun.

The summer was hot. The leaves on the lime trees in the Champs Elysées wilted in a short drought. The pavements were white and hot. Women wore their thinnest dresses, and many men shed their dark jackets. Julia found her work arduous. Then one day, after a heavy morning's work, about five in the afternoon, she gave way to the fatigue that spread over her like a cloak. After several attempts to keep awake, she spread her arms on the desk over the memo pad and fell into a deep sleep of exhaustion.

Paul found her there. His comings and goings were erratic these days. No one was ever sure when he would go out or come in, if indeed he were out. Entering the apartment he had found it oddly quiet. Marie of course slept in the afternoon. That was a cook's privilege. Gaston was out. He shopped twice a day, in the early morning at the public market, and after *déjeuner* for dry goods at the grocer's. But surely the typewriter should be clicking away? But no sound greeted him.

He went directly into the salon, and paused on the threshold, his hand on the doorknob. At first he did not see Julia for the sun had gone around to the west, and the salon which had been filled with golden sunshine in the morning was now in shadow.

For a long second a feeling of resentment stole over him that Julia had walked out on him on her own business. He felt slighted. Then he saw her. Was she ill? His heart stood still. He saw that she was sleeping quietly. He went over and stood looking down at her, and saw how her arms made an uncomfortable cushion for her head. Part of her cheek resting on the blotting pad. Her dark lashes, bronze-tipped, swept fanwise over her cheek. Her hair was tousled, and through the heat had stuck to her temples. Her neck, round and smooth, like a swan's, showed white and young above the low-cut collar of her dress. Her pen had fallen from limp fingers on to the carpet.

At first, with some alarm, Paul thought that she had fainted from the heat, and blamed himself for not having the forethought to provide her with a fan in anticipation of the heat wave. But when he bent to look more closely he saw that she was fast asleep. For the first time since he had known her he was aware of an acute feeling of compassion. She looked so defenceless that he had an urge to care for her. It was a new feeling, one that he never remembered having before even for Chantal who was enshrined in his heart for ever, who had treated him so badly, but whom he still loved. He thought Julia was uncomfortable lying on that hard pad. Surely she would be better off on the bed in her room. He acted at once upon this idea.

On impulse he opened the door then tiptoed past the kitchen and went to Julia's room at the end of the passage, and opened that door, too.

He returned to the salon, and bending, put his arms round her, gathering her up from the chair. Her head rolled grotesquely but she did not wake up. Her arms fell limply, but he held her close to him and went with catlike tread to her bedroom. Here he hesitated as though loath to put her down on the white bed. He was aware of the tininess of the room, of a heavy scent of flowers, but most of all he was aware of his burden. He looked down at her face for a long moment, at the silken fair hair on his coat sleeve, at her parted lips, revealing her white teeth. This was the closest he had ever been to her, and the knowledge moved him strangely.

He put her down gently, and raised a hand to lift the hair away from her face. He bent over her and again moved by some uncontrollable impulse he leant over her pressing his cheek against her hair. He was aware that his hands were trembling, and, too, he wanted to hold her close—closer to him again.

When he had shut the door he thought he might have kissed her. She would never know. His carrying her to her room had not disturbed Julia, but he recalled, with an exultant throb that she had turned her face towards him, nestling against his jacket, as seeking and finding comfort in his nearness.

He crept back to the salon, picked up the pen from the carpet and replaced it on the desk, then went into his room, where he changed and went out for the evening.

Paul never mentioned carrying Julia to her room. She never asked him. Only she knew. Only Marie was in the apartment, and certainly Marie was too fat to carry her even across a room. It could only be Paul. She knew by the way he avoided her that it was Paul, and if that were not sufficient pointer she guessed when an electric fan was delivered at the apartment and placed in position for her comfort. There was, too, in the ensuing days a noticeable easing off of work while the heat wave lasted.

At the end of five days of exceptionally torrid heat Paul came in one late afternoon, said he liked heat, but not tropical heat, and asked Julia if she would care to drive with him in the Bois.

She was wild with excitement. " Of course I'll go with you," she cried, her eyes shining and her cheeks flushed. " Just wait until I put on a clean dress."

To her astonishment, he, who was always so pernicketty,

said, "Don't bother, you look very nice as you are."

But she insisted on changing, and presently they drove down the Rue de Rivoli towards the Champs Elysées.

"What a lovely car," she admired.

"I ordered it at the Motor Show. I only took delivery a month ago."

The candles on the chestnut trees were over and the leaves full and heavy. Paul pointed out some of the sights, and Julia thought, He's almost human. She gave herself up to the enjoyment of the drive.

"Why are you so silent?" he asked, glancing at the quiet profile of his passenger.

"Am I? That's because I have never driven in this Bois before. It's an enchanting spot with all these lovely trees."

Paul drew up as near to the lake as he could.

"It is cooler here," he added lazily. They talked about the people in the boats on the lake, and then Paul said, "The season is nearly at an end when everybody will be leaving Paris for sea or country air. It'll be time to think of holidays."

Holidays! Julia had not thought of them. She did not want the old order to change. She waited, her heart beating fast, for Paul's next words. He said, "I shall be going on a business-cum-pleasure trip to Canada."

That shook Julia. She went white as she said, "That is a long way off."

"At least three thousand miles."

"Oh, how long do you expect to be away?"

"About a month."

"Isn't that a long holiday?"

"Long enough for me, but I want to think out some problems."

An upsurge of emotion brought a stinging sensation behind her eyes. She did not speak for a moment and then she said, "Is that why you brought me out here: to tell me that?"

"Oh no. I brought you out because it was hot and I

thought some fresh air would do us both good, so why not enjoy it together?"

" I see."

" No you don't, but you must believe me."

" Do I stay at the apartment while you are away?"

" Of course. Why not? Marie and Gaston will be there to take good care of you."

" Do they ever have a holiday?"

" Yes, when I return. I usually put up at an hotel while they are away. It is too uncomfortable without them, and if I have to get in a strange cook. Perhaps you, too, would like a short holiday? You may wish to go to London and see your friends."

" I lost them when I came here." She stirred herself to say, " I shall probably go to Biarritz."

" Why go there?"

" It is near to Spain and I might get the chance of crossing the frontier to see a bullfight."

" You'd hate that."

" How do you know what I hate, or for that matter what I love?"

" I don't," he admitted, " but most women loathe bullfights."

" Then I shall bathe."

" Alone?"

" Perhaps not." It was a provocative answer.

" Don't bathe at Biarritz; it is too dangerous," he warned her earnestly.

" There are lifeguards."

" The sea is always rough. Great rollers come rushing in from the Atlantic."

" In other words you don't want me to go away. You are full of objections."

He paused before he agreed soberly—" No, I do not wish you to go. I prefer you to stay at the apartment with Gaston and Marie because I know that you will be safe with them."

" I don't understand," she said in perplexity.

c

"And I can't explain—not now. But I do understand that a holiday is needful. You must play to come back ready for hard work in the autumn."

She flashed, "I don't want to have a holiday with that in view. It might surprise you, monsieur, to hear that I do not *like* work. I hate it. I work as a means to an end. I have to work to live and that is all there is to it."

Julia sounded as bitter as Monsieur often was. She was hurt that he was going away and leaving her, uncaring what was happening to her, probably thinking her safe in Gaston and Marie's care.

Paul teased, "You are full of surprises, Miss Brown."

"Not to those who really know me."

"Why do you wish to shut me out?"

"Because you are not really interested," she told him daringly, then waited for his cold disclaimer.

"Then *you* don't know *me*, for I am interested in everybody," he said and his tone was certainly not cold.

Julia was puzzled. She felt sick with the heat, and she was full of disappointment at hearing that Monsieur meant to go away for a whole month to Canada, and she wondered how she could live through four weeks of loneliness. Not that he was much of a companion but he broke the daylight hours for her. Sometimes, in a kind mood, and they had been more frequently lately, he made her day for her. Whatever his mood Monsieur was never dull. She wanted to tell him he had spoilt her drive this afternoon by announcing his journey to Canada, but there were some things it would be tactless to say. He would wish he had not asked her out. It was Paul who said to her in an aggrieved tone, "I thought we were going to relax here in the shade, but your threat to holiday at Biarritz worries me. I am anything but relaxed. Supposing you do go, and bathe and get drowned—"

"What of it?" she demanded recklessly.

"What should I do for a secretary?"

"Find a new one. There are dozens going."

"Dozens like you?" he asked whimsically.

" Much better—nicer, clever, more *chic*—"

" I wonder. Yet oddly it is you that I want."

The remark made her feel happier—not that she believed all Paul said. He could be as nice as possible when he liked, only he did not often like.

There was a deep regret in her heart, too, for since she had been living in the cosy apartment where everything spelt of money, yet with the luxury and taste that often goes with it, and seen Monsieur on his " own ground," it had seemed that he was a man she could like very much. He had not shown her his best side. Indeed, he appeared to delight in showing her his worst, but she had seen him with friends, business, and cultured academic people. She had, too, been told more than once that he was once cheerful and gay, and she began to wish desperately that she had the power over him to recall that carefree gaiety that was in his past, and could, with the right girl come to life in the present. He was a romantic, too. Julia had known boys in her own recent past, but they had never measured up to her fastidious taste. There was always something wrong, or they fell short of her heart's requirements, that indefinable quality in a man which appeals so strongly to women. She felt that Monsieur did fit in, or he would do so if only she could find the right key to unlock his heart. Inwardly she had responded to him as soon as they met, in spite of his repellent attitude to her. It had seemed like a cloak, a pretence, a kind of screen that hid the real man's heart. Of course Julia knew what was wrong. And if only Paul would give a hint she might be quick enough to seize it and turn it to good account for their joint happiness, but Monsieur hugged his secrets and was often unapproachable. Julia was never able to reach even a friendly status with him. If only she had the power to create a new interest in Monsieur's life, how happy she would be.

Of course Paul knew nothing of these thoughts which occurred to Julia at odd moments during the day and wakeful spells in the night. Tonight was one of the odd daily moments as she sat quietly beside him, her eyes dreamy, seeing yet not observing the passing sights. He gave his mind to driving his fast car for it was between lights and the rush hour, when he needed all his wits about him.

Having skirted the Arc de Triomphe they raced down the Champs Elysées where the cafés were lighted up, the evening customers filling their pavement tables, and the traffic was intense.

And so to the block of apartments where Paul lived.

" Thank you for a lovely drive, monsieur," Julia said with an odd mixture of deference and politeness, though she would have liked to cry enthusiastically, " It has been wonderful sitting beside you. I only wish we could have gone on like this forever." But Paul wouldn't have understood her gushing remarks.

He helped her out saying, " Thank *you*, Miss Brown. It is one of the most delightful hours I have spent for a long while, not so much because I am a true Parisian and love the Bois, and I think you do, too, but because I have been with you. I feel quite relaxed."

He spoke in French, and it wasn't because he was " het up." Never before had Julia thought what a wonderful language it was, so musical, so caressing. Paul's tone was soft too, low and intimate a though he were speaking of love.

Julia walked up the steps to the marble-paved hall in a bemused state, forgetting in her spiritual state of mind to reply to the janitor who bade them a civil, " *Bon soir, M'sieu' et Dame.*"

Chapter Five

AT LAST Fate stepped in to take a hand in shaping Julia's affairs, and gave her the chance she had been longing for, but not in the guise she had expected. She was feeling a bit limp, and in one way looking forward to a few days' peace after the last four months' drive, when Monsieur's turbulent personality would leave the apartment for a while. She would feel terribly lonely of course, and had no idea how she would last out the weeks alone, but she needed a couple of days to adjust herself and to gather her ragged forces together.

With a feeling that everything must be as tidy for Monsieur's going as it would be for his homecoming, Julia turned out the bottom drawer of the desk, and came upon several items that must have been the property of her predecessor.

It seemed strange to her that a girl called Chantal, a name which surely spelled romance, should collect such mundane things as a reel of cotton, a lucky charm, and a poem. This last was written in French, in Monsieur's handwriting. Julia had read a line of the poem before she realised that it was meant solely for Chantal. Then she put it down quickly feeling dizzy and faint.

She paused longing to read what Monsieur had written. It came to Julia then that she had a right to read what Paul, the lover, thought of love, that loving him herself she must know what he would write to her some day. It was a dream of course. It could never be, but oh, how wonderful, if it could!

She toyed with the paper, opening it, then folding it up again. The temptation grew . . . Deliberately she spread the paper on the blotter and read through the poem. If Julia's gesture was defiant, it did not last. She was in tears when she came to the end of the poem.

She recalled one line which caught her imagination more than the rest. Paul wrote,

" My darling, how I long to run my fingers through your silken hair . . ."

Julia could imagine him doing this. She cried unrestrainedly for a little while.

With an effort, for by now she had memorised the lines, she folded up the piece of paper and put it on the top of the desk with the other small things. With that gesture came a sense of guilt. She had done a wicked thing. She had spied on Paul, and trespassed on his property to satisfy her own curiosity. She felt hot with shame. Now would come the terrible moments when she would have to own up to spying, and she was afraid how he would react. He would be furious. It was inevitable that she would get the sack. Her own inquisitiveness was her downfall. She would be punished by never being able to see Paul again. She wept in self-pity for a long time.

Presently, when Julia felt able to go on and the dizziness passed, her mind was clear, and the tears wiped from her eyes by the back of her hand, and she was able to finish clearing the drawer, she came to a small leather box. She opened it slowly, aware that this was a " ring " case, well aware too, that she might see something which would affect her even more than the poem had done.

She was shocked and amazed to see a ring. The box was lined with white velvet and in a small division was tucked the loveliest emerald ring Julia had ever seen. She gasped. She could only stare at the large green stone surrounded by diamonds. She turned it slowly and the facets caught the sun, glittering and sparkling with a gaiety no cheap jewel could hope to have.

Obviously this was an engagement ring, the one Monsieur had given to Chantal less than a year ago, and which she must have returned to him before her flight. Otherwise how did it get here? Monsieur, in a fit of rage, must have thrust it away in a drawer and forgotten it. Julia felt she could conjecture for a long while, yet not get at the truth. She would have to give it to him for obviously it was a valuable ring.

Monsieur had said, " Throw all that rubbish away," but the ring and the poem were not rubbish.

She closed the case with care, her heart beating fast, and put it on the top of the desk. She was uneasy about reminding him of a closed chapter in his life, for had not Andrew told her that Chantal had run away with another man? Yet she could not leave it about, much less throw it away. For the moment she hid the case behind a cardboard box.

Paul came in. He was in a good mood, and Julia's heart sank because of the blow she had to deal him.

He said, "One last big spree before I go. I am taking a party to Chantilly the day after tomorrow. You will of course join us, Miss Brown."

Julia nodded absentmindedly because her thoughts were not so much on what Paul was saying as on the ring lying snugly in its case within arm's length.

"You can't make the excuse that you have no clothes," Paul told her smilingly.

"No, I have a nice new dress that I shall wear if the weather is fine."

"It will be. All the weather experts say so."

They both laughed as at a joke. Then Paul's eye fell on the reel of cotton, the lucky charm, and the folded piece of worn paper. "Hello, what on earth are these?" he inquired. Clearly he had forgotten the paper. "Don't hoard rubbish, Miss Brown. Throw it all away."

Julia swept the charm and reel into the wastepaper basket, then she said with a quiet deliberation that focused his attention, "I think this paper is of some importance to you. It is written in your handwriting."

Paul picked it up and opened it.

For a moment he scanned the paper in silence, then with a sharp exclamation he tore it into a hundred pieces, until no two letters were left together. These fell like snowflakes on the reel and charm already in the basket.

"I suppose you've read it?" he asked savagely.

Julia's eyes were enormous with fear as she nodded. "Yes, monsieur, I have."

"Though you knew it was not for your eyes?"

"Yes. I am sorry. It was a terrible thing to do."

His reaction was unexpected. She thought he would have loathed her for reading the poem. Instead he advised, "Forget that you have done so. Such rubbish should never have been kept."

Julia said with some spirit, "I didn't think it was rubbish. I—liked it."

"It was never meant for you."

" I know. No man has ever been moved to write poetry to me."

She saw that his face was working strangely. Its expression frightened her. Yet she was emboldened to say, " It is one of the loveliest poems I have ever read." Her voice broke a little with emotion.

" Is that why you have been crying?"

Julia drew a long breath. She wanted to lie, to say there was nothing to cry about, to pretend that she was as bitter as he was, but it was of no use. The telltale signs of tears were still on her face.

She said simply, " I cried because—I pitied you."

" Pity did you say?"

" Yes, you gave her so much of yourself, and obviously she wasn't worth it. You are still worshipping an idol, one who always had feet of clay."

Paul did not reply, only continued to stare at her, but now his face was not frightening.

She persisted, a feeling of fear sweeping through her. " And this case: there is a valuable ring in it. Perhaps you will take care of it."

His expression changed. " What is the point of asking me to look after it? I don't want the thing. When I said throw everything away in the drawer, I meant it. I had forgotten this ring, but even had I remembered it I should still say, throw it away. I bought it for a purpose, and the purpose no longer exists."

He spoke in French and she could hear the cold fury in his measured tones. As he spoke he picked up the velvet case and threw it into the basket where it was lost amid scraps of poem.

Julia stared aghast. " Please don't do that," she begged. " It is wrong for anyone to throw away a valuable ring. Take it. If you don't want to see it and be reminded of unpleasant things then lock it in your safe. You will only regret your hastiness."

" I doubt that."

Julia stooped swiftly, and rooting about among the papers picked out the case. "Take it," she urged in a shaking voice nearly in tears.

"I will not. You take care of it. I don't care."

She slipped it into a top drawer. "You can have it later," she said; "not now, when you are so angry."

"I believe you wanted it for yourself all the time."

Julia drew herself up. "You mistake me, monsieur," she told him coldly. "You must be crazy to want the janitor to have it."

Paul was silent. Then Julia said, "It is an engagement ring, isn't it?"

"It was: so what?"

"It is very beautiful. You have good taste, monsieur."

"I chose it for the loveliest girl in France."

"I am sure you did. Then misfortune came."

"How do you know?"

"Someone told me."

"So you have known all along that I am a man without a heart because a cheat broke it?"

Julia said vigorously, "No, monsieur, you are not that weak. And even if we believe in broken hearts, we must believe, too, that they mend."

"No."

"I do not agree. You might like to give this ring some day to another girl?"

"Who would want secondhand goods?"

"I wish you would not pretend to be so hard, monsieur."

Paul laughed. "Pretend!" he echoed, then broke off to ask, "Aren't you taking all this too much to heart? This is my private trouble and nothing to do with you. Yet you drag my secret out into the open and dare to give me advice on what to do."

"I don't know anything you do not wish to tell me. I would not presume to give advice. I only know that it grieves me to see you so unhappy, and I should like to help you if I could."

" How? I wish you knew, too. I would give a great deal to forget."

" There must be a way of helping you."

Paul smiled. He said in a kindlier tone, " Thank you for your interest in me." Then he said, " Give me the case. I will put it in my safe. Does that please you?"

Julia was relieved. " Yes, it does."

Julia often met Andrew in the evenings. He did not come to the flat for her now because his coming annoyed Paul, who went out of his way to speak to Andrew with what Julia described as a " patient civility," which she and Andrew found irritating. Both guessed that Paul's manner hid a dislike of the situation that Paul would or could not express without giving something away. Paul had never asked Andrew in even for a drink, though he was not mean over entertaining. Andrew would have been stupid not to see that Paul did not like him, and so he arranged with Julia to meet her either downstairs in the vestibule, or in a little café-restaurant around the corner. Unknown to Paul, Andrew's main idea in meeting Julia so often was to find out how she was getting on with Paul.

" For heaven's sake don't go out of your way to rile him. Make him feel pleased with himself. Keep him in a good temper," he would urge while they ate at a secluded table inside the café where passers-by would not see them.

At first Julia had demanded a reason for this saying, " I'm not a lion tamer," or " What do you expect me to do?"

Andrew had been cagey about taking her into his confidence. Julia had a direct way of looking at a man as though she were probing his secrets. She made him feel embarrassed. In the end he decided to confide in her. He admitted that there was a chance of Paul putting money into their family company and pulling it together, before it was too late.

" Why approach Monsieur's company in the beginning? Couldn't you have found someone else to help?"

" That was coincidence, Fate."

" Why should he especially help you?" she demanded, though her heart had contracted with fear, for she did not want her uncle and cousins to suffer if she could help it. Also she did not want Monsieur to come into her personal affairs.

" To make money for himself, of course."

" But Monsieur is a rich man."

" As I mentioned before that is one reason why he *is* rich. He has capital to play with."

" I know."

Andrew said, " He is very successful at it. He could help and he would, especially as you are living in his apartment. He has an extra urge to do it."

" What?"

Andrew paused before he said deliberately, " He might want to please you."

Julia scoffed at the idea. " That would be his last reason for helping. Monsieur has never shown the least desire to please me."

" Then why don't you try to please him first?"

" I wouldn't know how," she told Andrew flatly. " His servants give him all the creature comforts he can possibly want. He is ambitious and his mind is centred on money, especially now that his heart is dead. I might have had a go once—but no, I couldn't have touched his heart, even then, he was obsessed by the other girl."

" I know. I told you about her. But that's all in the past. I once read a poem in which it said, ' Dead men rise up never.' Substitute love for men and it is as true."

Julia nodded, " I've read it and the morbid ending, ' And even the weariest river winds somewhere safe to the sea.' " Then she went on in her smooth voice, " Why don't you call on him and state your personal case frankly? He is often bad-tempered but he is just and can be reasonable."

" Because for some reason he has taken a violent dislike

to me. He was prejudiced against me from the start."

" How absurd! Why? What have you done or said to him to make him hate you?"

" He doesn't think I am a good friend for you. He feels I dominate you."

" What utter rubbish! I have a mind of my own. I don't need a mentor."

" Perhaps he feels I am using you as a kind of stooge and resents it."

She smiled suddenly, " Monsieur would not be able to keep that one in. He would have hurled that accusation back at me like a stone."

" Of course I may be wrong, but he may even think we are in love with each other."

" But Andrew, don't be silly, you are my cousin. You've been like a brother to me since I was a tot."

" Well, cousins marry, you know."

" Yes, but—oh, it is absurd."

" If only he would see me and voice his suspicions I could put him right at once. Me must be aware that our firm has applied to his for aid. We are trying to open negotiations, and though they haven't actually refused to negotiate, there is an unnecessary interminable delay in getting a move on that is driving me crazy."

" If you are patient it will all come right," she soothed.

" You haven't seen any documents lying around?"

" No, but we don't deal with the main firm's business at the apartment. Anyhow, Monsieur would never dream of leaving private papers about. If the commissioner brings along any private papers for him to work on during an evening he keeps them in the safe in his bedroom." Then she said sharply, " But what if I have seen a folder in the apartment? Andrew, you aren't suggesting I should search Monsieur's room, find any papers that concern you and tell you what is in them?"

He made no reply, and she went on, her eyes dark with trouble, " I always thought I could trust you—oh, Andrew!

Surely you must know that I could not betray his trust."

They had parted early, and when Julia said " good night," in the vestibule her voice was cold. She had the feeling they could never be friends again, and she felt, too, terribly lonely.

As Julia let herself into the apartment Paul met her in the hall.

One quick glance at his face showed that his mood was serious and thoughtful. She said immediately, " Have you been waiting? Do you want me to take a note?"

He shook his head, fixed his eyes pensively on her face as though he would read her thoughts, and said, " Not to-night. What made you think I did?"

" You seemed thoughtful as though you were turning over some business in your mind."

" Well, I was—"

" Can I be of any help? Most of the papers have gone to the office."

The question was perfunctory. Anyhow Monsieur knew that all papers of consequence had been sent to the main office for safe keeping while he was away. To her surprise he replied, " Perhaps you can."

He opened the door of the salon and they went in. The room was silent and a little stuffy. She had opened the window when she left earlier in the evening, but Gaston must have gone in and shut it. He had the French mania for close atmospheres.

" Sit down," he invited. And when she did so he opened the box of cigarettes and offered it to her.

" No thank you."

" Would you like a drink?"

" No thank you."

" I am going to mix you one all the same. I want one myself."

He did not speak for a while but mixed a drink and poured the contents of the jug into two glasses, and handed one to her. Then he sat down and lighted a cigarette with

maddening deliberation and puffed away at it before asking
suddenly,

" When you were out with your cousin tonight—pardon,
you were out with Andrew Lester, were you not?"

Julia nodded, her face as serious as his now, she seemed
pale and her eyes were enormous. A hint of what was
coming had occurred to her, and secretly she was in a panic,
not knowing how best to answer him. " Yes—"

" Do you meet often?"

" About twice a week, sometimes three times, as this
week."

" You are very friendly with each other?"

" Naturally."

" I see." But Paul already knew all that. He was worried.
He longed to trust her, but he had to find out, to know
whether she was speaking the truth. So he asked her questions of which he knew the answers. Then he said, " I suppose, being business people, interested in your own company,
you discuss various problems connected with business?"

Julia sat up, her mind suddenly alert. Monsieur was probing her with a definite purpose. She thought, How much
does he know about my friendship with Andrew? Has he
seen us in the café around the corner? But of course he has.
Why was he questioning her so relentlessly, like a cross-
examiner? What could she admit with tact? What indeed
was there to admit which might have a bad effect on those
relations that Andrew was working to establish between the
company and Monsieur's?

She said as quietly as she could, " I don't think we *discuss* the problems arising in our family business, but Andrew
has certainly mentioned that our firm has serious troubles."
They had begun talking in English, but now subconsciously
Paul had continued in French, and Julia copied him.

" You do not talk about my business?"

" Only generally and in passing."

" That leads to another question that has come to my
mind. Please do not be angry; but did you know that I might

be useful to your family business when you came to see me at the Hilton Hotel regarding the post of private secretary?"

Julia felt faint with humiliation. That he should ask her such a question! Gathering all her strength to meet this question she forced herself to reply calmly, but her fists were shut so tightly her fingernails dug into the palms of her hands.

"I had no idea who or what you were. I was keen on going abroad because any adventure appealed to me. I did not inquire about you personally, only Miss Catchpole spoke of you with awe. To be fair to Andrew, he did not know either. Later, when he was worried about my safety he made some inquiries about you. More as a man than what your business was, and he told me then that you helped sick companies. It was *after* that that Andrew heard from my uncle that our firm was not doing too well." Then she said in a hurt tone that quavered with a breakdown in her manner, "You don't think I have been disloyal to you, Monsieur?"

"No-o. That is, I try not to think so. That is not your fault perhaps. You are the victim of another's disloyalty. Once before, when I trusted someone I thought I knew well implicitly, I found that under an innocent and apparently frank manner she was being most untrustworthy and disloyal. Though I am well aware that for one black sheep there are thousands of white, I find it difficult to trust anyone again. Now I want to trust you. I do. But occasionally there is a foolish doubt."

Julia knew whom Monsieur meant, and she said, her tears passing, "It is foolish of you to doubt me."

"I know. Forgive me. I do not deserve that you should be so frank with me. But I do not trust your cousin. Perhaps you do not realise why he is in Paris, but I do."

"Yes, I know."

"Then you are not aware that he works hard to contact me?"

"Andrew has mentioned that, too."

"You may be surprised to hear that he would like you

to be a go-between between my company and himself?"

Julia wanted to lie, but with those fierce probing eyes on her face she found it difficult to do so, even though she well knew what telling the truth would mean, and might rouse Monsieur's everlasting anger towards her. She wished with all her heart that Andrew had never mentioned his problems and dragged her into them, for now surely he was writing "finis" to the lovely hopes she had been harbouring lately in her heart.

She said in a low voice, "I guessed that tonight."

Paul drew a long breath. "Did it annoy you?"

"I was furious. I am still. It has spoilt my feelings for Andrew."

"What sort of feelings? Come, Miss Brown, I must know."

"Our friendship."

"Why do you wish to prolong this hurt? Why don't you answer straightforwardly? Are you in love with this fine cousin of yours?"

How harshly he spoke! Why should she reply? What business was it of his his? Yet she heard herself saying,

"No, monsieur."

"Are you sure?" His voice was not so insistent. "He is handsome in a way that women like. He relies on a woman for his comfort. He does not appear strong. There is appeal for a woman to take care of him. Some men are like that, kind and gentle as I could not hope to be. Why do you not love him, Miss Brown?"

He rose in agitation, adding abruptly, "Finish your drink. It must be warm and mawkish by now. I will mix another."

Julia did not reply. Perhaps he did not expect her to. His back was towards her as he mixed another drink. She saw his hand though. It was shaking badly. She glanced around her at the familiar room with its cosy decorations and that sense of comfort and well-being which rich colours can give. She saw the disarrangement in it, portending change. He was about to leave it, and already some of his baggage, ready locked and strapped was piled up by the door. The waste-paper basket was full, spilling over on to the floor. An assortment of sticks and a large coloured umbrella lay athwart the arms of a large chair.

As he turned, her eyes, swimming now in tears, came back to him. The glasses, full of amber liquid, were in his hands. His eyes met hers. She saw that his were stormy, turbulent and questioning. He demanded challengingly, "Why?" He held out a glass to Julia who took the slender stem between her fingers.

"Drink it up and then answer me, Miss Brown."

Glass in hand he began to pace the room restlessly. Then, as though afraid of hearing something he would not like, he suggested, "Take your time. We have all night before us."

Julia obeyed. She drank some of the mixture. It was as before but more potent, and was like fire going down her throat. She gasped. "This is terribly strong."

"It will do you good."

He stopped before her, then swallowed his drink at a gulp, putting the glass down on the table with such force that the stem broke in half, when he threw the pieces impatiently on to the tray.

"Well?"

She spoke quietly. "I have never even thought of loving Andrew in that way, monsieur."

Paul drew a long breath, a curious sibilance that fell like a hiss across the quiet of the room. Julia added, and now instead of the relief which had drawn forth that strange noise, Paul held his breath, his nerves tense. "Go on," he ordered.

"I could not do so now because for a long while I have been in love with someone else. He fills my whole heart."

Julia thought wearily, The battle is over. Now he knows. It is up to him. But I can't fight against him any longer. If I am sent away then I must try to bear my loss somehow, but I can't go on seeing him every day, being close to him, and getting nowhere. But Paul did not react as she had expected.

When she spoke he went pale, and for a moment it seemed as though he had lost his grip on himself. He tried to mouth a few words, but no sound passed his lips. He went over to her desk, his back towards her, so that she should not see him striving for self-control, hiding his emotions from her, struggling for calm.

Then suddenly he swung round to face her and the words that had tried so hard to be uttered came out in a spate and he shouted angrily to her.

" The impertinence! How dare you sit there quietly telling me you are in love with some other unnamed man. I shall not allow this kind of thing to go on under my nose."

She looked at him wide-eyed and innocent. " You asked me, monsieur, otherwise I should not have told you my secret, for it is mine and not yours," she cried in a voice that shook badly.

" How did it happen? Where did you meet this fellow? Is he one of my friends? Have you been carrying on with one of my friends under my nose? Those roses—I remember now, roses mean love."

" It isn't one of your friends, monsieur. I have not heard from the señor since those roses came. Please don't spoil my love story. It is just one of those things that happen. I could not help it. Indeed, I did not realise what had come to me until it was too late."

Paul was stunned. He was perplexed. He passed a worried hand over his head as though to clear the cobwebs that cluttered his brain.

He came to stand in front of her, looking down at her with a kind of longing in his eyes. He observed that she sat there white and trembling, and an unusual pity for her moved him. He who had so little pity to give nowadays was deeply touched, for did not he, too, know those dreadful pangs of unrequited love?

He said, " There, don't get so upset. It shall pass. Do

not grieve. You are young, and there are bound to be more chances for love for you in the future. I am so sorry. I should not have spoken as I did, for I am not entirely insensitive, but I, too, have my torment, and something within often urges me to hurt others as I am hurt, yet nowhere do I find any relief but in work and time. You see, I know exactly all about this crisis you are going through. It is not new. I am told that most people in their quest for love and happiness go through one or more of such crises before they find what they are seeking. But why am I telling you all this? Now go to bed."

Julia rose obediently. She was glad to leave him before he could ask her any more confounding questions. She was glad, too, that he had not seen the point of her fatal remark, that he was the man she was in love with. He had mistaken her, but for how long she did not know. With luck the truth might not dawn on him until there was a world of space between them.

She walked unsteadily to the door, her legs light and disobedient.

Paul helped her to her room. " Good night, Miss Brown. Get to bed quickly. Remember, tomorrow is another day."

She giggled a little. " The day of the races, monsieur."

" Yes, and you must look your best. Be ready at eleven, please, Miss Brown."

It was only afterwards that it occurred to Julia that she and Monsieur had spoken to each other in French. He had understood what she said, while she had been at ease with all those idioms which had so far proved a stumbling block to her progress. She undressed quickly and got into bed, her mind a mixture of happiness and sadness. When she thought of the next month she was sad. She would not be seeing Paul daily, and she had no idea what to do with herself until he came home and she would hear his familiar voice again, and who knew what lovely Canadian girl would fall for him or he fall for her while he was there. She was happy, too, in a way because now she would have time to see her love and friendship for him in better perspective. She must learn to govern the fear for him that always raised its head at his approach, wondering at his mood, her brain working overtime conjuring up ways to meet his mood, her nerves desperately tense. So perhaps this parting will be for the best for me, she thought.

Chapter Six

NEXT MORNING Marie woke Julia early. " There is much to do before eleven o'clock, M'm'selle," she said happily. " For you must not keep M'sieu waiting. My niece will be here at nine. She expects to be so busy."

From that moment Julia's end of the flat was in turmoil. Marie's niece surpassed herself with making the dress Julia wanted to wear at the races. It was of Rose du Barri brocade, with dramatic huge puffed short sleeves with a clever effect of slimming over the hips. Not that Julia needed to look thinner, but the narrow skirt balanced the wide sleeves.

So pleased was Marie's niece with the dress that she brought her hairdresser-husband to arrange Julia's fair hair into a new upswept coiffure. She had borrowed a wide brimmed black hat from one of the models also some black accessories. She also brought from the atelier a half-bottle of Dior toilet water which Julia thought heavenly, and not so cloying as scent.

When Julia was dressed, Marie and Gaston were called in to see the finished product.

"*Ravissante! Trés belle! P'tite Mignonne!*" These and Marie's wide range of admiring adjectives were said many times. Marie clasped her hands in ecstasy. She posed in other prayerful attitudes, delighted that at long last M'm'selle was going to the races in a dress fit for a Queen to wear.

In the middle of this praise and adulation, the door bell rang, and Gaston, with a hurried cry, " The guests! " ran to answer the door.

The women paused to listen. Men's voices, men out to play for the day, laughing freely, shedding inhibitions, cracking jokes, came from the hall, and moved slowly into the salon where there was a table of drinks. Girls were there, too, their voices clear as crystal, more staccato and excited than the men's.

Julia heard Monsieur's voice, and the clink of glasses. Paul sounded cheerful. She heard her name, and understood they were waiting for her appearance.

Presently Gaston, his eyes shining, came hurrying along the passage, saying, " *Vite, M'm'selle!* "

" Just coming," she said. Julia kissed Marie and her niece, for were they not responsible for her enjoyment? " Am I all right?"

" It is perfect, M'm'selle. Nevaire 'ave I seen one so—so *ravissante!* " in that strange " pidgin " English and French she had learned from Julia.

They followed, an admiring entourage, as far as the door of the salon, whispering words of praise and encouragement.

The door was open and for a moment Julia paused on the threshold, her eyes seeking Monsieur's, wondering what he would think about her get-up. As in a dream Julia saw the effect of her entrance on the other people in the room. It seemed full of people, men and women, and the atmosphere

was thick with exotic scents. The effect of her entrance was
electric. One moment everyone was talking and laughing,
then suddenly, at sight of Julia, there was a sudden
hush.

Behind Julia Marie and her niece exchanged delighted
glances. They listened openly to the shower of compliments
that cracked through that first silence following Julia's
appearance, and before a murmur of approbation broke out.

Paul was the first to detach himself from the group of
guests, and though his eyes lighted up with a strange look,
a kind of flame behind the brown which made Julia's own
eyes fall, he did not smile. It was not an approving look. The
word that fell from his lips was the one she had heard many
times already this morning, *Ravissante*!

"Marie's niece has done well." His voice said he was very
proud of her.

He turned back to the table, well knowing that it would
be forsaken, for the men were already crowding around Julia,
complimenting her extravagantly, admiring her and her
clothes. They were not too effusive as they would have liked
to be, for word had gone round the clubs they haunted that
Paul was possessive and jealous of his latest secretary. Money
had given him power, and they knew that if anyone crossed
him in a personal matter like this *affaire*, he would be ruthless in breaking even his closest friend. So they tempered
their admiration for this lovely girl with the golden blonde
hair and the brown velvet eyes, and who wore her clothes
with a Frenchwoman's *chic*. They were content to wait
until Paul was out of the way before joining that court of
admirers which would buzz round her like bees throughout
the day.

Under this flattery Julia opened out like a flower.

She was delighted to have drawn such an expression as
"adorable" from the reserved Paul. Obviously her dress
and the spontaneous admiration of his friends had pleased
him for his grave mood seemed to disappear and he became
a gay and witty host, urbane and genial as Julia had never

seen him, but which was, according to Marie talking about M'sieu' later, exactly as Paul used to be.

It was Paul who arranged in which cars his guests should go to Chantilly. Julia was delighted to find herself in Paul's car. No one could have planned it so cleverly or indeed so openly, as Monsieur, for girls liked him and most of them clamoured frankly to sit beside him. Paul was blunt to rudeness in refusing their company, and unfortunately that caused them to dislike the secretary. Sulky girls in lovely clothes are not pretty.

When Julia, to keep the peace, suggested going in one of the other cars, Paul told her sharply, " You will do as I tell you, Miss Brown."

Julia tossed her head and laughed. " Supposing I prefer to go in another car?"

" In that case—go," he said abruptly and without humour. Then seeing that she was teasing him he said, " You will go with me."

Paul chose another girl to sit beside him and indicated to Julia that she should sit in the back with another man who was a non-stop talker and could be relied upon to pull his weight with a quiet partner.

So Julia did not speak much to Paul on the way partly because it would have meant distracting the driver but also because she had to give attention to what her own partner was saying.

Julia looked for a while out of the window nearest her at the passing scene, and the environs of Paris with its shuttered plastered houses and cobble-stoned streets and cafés sheltering under lime trees, all of which she knew very little.

Paul was a fast driver.

And so out of Paris through green forests and to the pretty racecourse where everything, even the buildings, was painted a glossy white.

The sun shone brilliantly in a cloudless sky, the grass was a lush green, and there were flowers everywhere. Traffic was thick near the racecourse, and they were forced to slow down and take their turn with other racegoers. The scene was not new to Paul who made a hobby of racegoing as an antidote to money making. Paul found relaxation in all the sights and smells, the noise of the mob, the clamour of bells and cheering. Every time was fresh to him, and today because Julia was there and her dress and stunning good looks were creating a furore, and he was the envy of all men, Paul found it more refreshing than ever.

There were moments on the way down when passing shadows obscured the amazing glow of happiness that Julia wore like an aura about her, for she was with Paul and her clothes were right and she felt a credit to him. But there were other forces to be reckoned with, for instance the extremely pretty girl who sat beside him and demanded some of his attention, and who let it be known by little mannerisms and an air of possession, that she was Paul's friend and he had chosen her to sit beside him.

In the excitement of today Julia knew that she was inclined to forget that tomorrow Paul would be far away from France. She was reminded afresh at a hold up in the traffic, when the girl sitting beside him in the seat of honour asked Paul in her high-pitched voice, " What line are you flying with tomorrow?"

" French. I leave my apartment at dawn. It seems a less fatiguing line than most."

" I shall fly out by the same line next week."

" I should advise you to. It has a good name, with no blemish on its record."

So this girl would be seeing Paul in Canada! Julia felt sick at the thought. They talked more or less intimately for a while, but as the traffic block resolved itself then, Julia could not hear what they were saying.

Directly they arrived and were taken to Paul's box where lunch was laid in a small retiring room behind the open box. They had lunch at one large round table. The flower decorations were superb.

Julia had no idea who arranged the names on the place

cards in front of each cover at the table, but she found herself opposite Paul, and in direct line of his vision. Every time she looked up it was to find his eyes fixed on her. Sometimes he smiled as their eyes met, and her heart was warmed by his friendliness. She strove to please Paul further by taking an interest in the men on either side of her. But oddly when she was in her gayest mood and thought Paul must be delighted with her, he did not smile, but with a wooden expression his eyes shied away from her as from a stranger.

After lunch, when Paul was able to leave his guests to themselves, he whispered to Julia, " Now we will go down to the paddock, watch the horses parade and mark your card. You'll want to place some small bets, too."

" I'm not betting today. I have no money to lose."

" You must bet. It is part of the fun of racing. I'll help you mark your card. You can borrow from me for your first race and pay me back later."

" Supposing I lose?" But she rose to go with him and side by side they went towards the paddock.

" Too bad! You must try again. You are bound to have beginner's luck and win. By the end of the afternoon you shall have enough to line a nest egg ready for your next racing day."

So there was to be another day like this! Then her face clouded. " That is a long time off. I can't go until you return, and then the season may be over, or you will be too busy to go."

It required little pressure to make Julia accept some money for betting, partly because she guessed Paul wanted to put her in debt to him, and she did not wish to spoil his last day.

As they made their way to the paddock several times Paul raised his hat to friends and acquaintances who seemed to go out of their way to greet him. Occasionally they paused for a few words, though Paul did not encourage dallying. Once he suggested wryly, " Perhaps I should carry my hat. My arm aches taking it off so many times."

" Is it always like this?" she asked in amusement.

" Oh no, this is a special day because you are with me. One of the best-dressed women here this afternoon."

That was not true, but it was pleasant to hear.

It was soon obvious to Paul though that whether she walked in the paddock or stood at the white rails to watch the horses parade before a race, or gossiped idly in the club enclosure, Julia was followed by a train of admirers who seized every opportunity to get a close up of her face. Press photographers quickly found her photogenic. This was noticeable even when she sat in Paul's flower decorated box watching the actual races. It was one of the largest of the owner-boxes, the men who kept racing going, and was comfortable and roomy, and in one of the best positions for viewing.

Paul knew that his name was on most men's lips today. Last time it had been like this Chantal queened it in his box. Today it was the English miss, Julia. The crowd kept asking, " Who is she? Where did he find her? Look what Paul's got! She's the prettiest and smartest blonde on the Course."

Paul was thoroughly amiable today. He had promised himself that nothing should disturb the last fling of enjoyment before he flew off to Canada in the morning. He owned a string of racehorses and was well known to stewards, trainers and jockeys, but today he had no horse running. No one bothered him for tips, but all his friends longed to be introduced to Julia. He was happy, too, that men envied him Julia with her spectacular beauty of brown eyes and blonde hair. They envied his luck, his taste and that he had the good fortune to indulge it. It was not so much that Julia was lovelier than many other women, or even more attractive than other members of his party, the girls chosen for their looks, and certainly Julia could not hold a candle to Chantal who was born outwardly with ' the lot,' and who was so breathtakingly lovely that there was never any question of competition. But Julia shone with a strange inward glow. There was a touching simplicity about her, an astonishing youthfulness that was a sure attraction for the jaded appetites of those successful tycoons whose money could and did skin the markets of the world of their loveliest girls. The trouble with those was that they never stuck to one girl, but tired so soon and were always seeking change. Paul thought men would never tire of Julia because they were sure there would always be some new discovery which she must keep hidden instinctively as a reserve.

As Paul advised her about her card, their heads were often together. She won several races, repaid her debt to him, to his secret annoyance, and said happily that her purse was bursting with money. " All due to your cleverness, Monsieur."

As host he could not be with her all the time, but he managed to make many spare moments, missing some of the races, because he was looking at her instead. He was not always at her side. Sometimes he stood in a crowd behind her. Even if she wandered off with others he seemed to know where she had gone. Once he focused his glasses on the crowd he found her easily, for her personality caused Julia to stand out in a crowd. He seldom ' lost ' her. She was like a magnet to him.

There was a glittering quality about Julia today. She had determined not to think of tomorrow, when Paul would be gone. Time for tears then. She was glad that Paul had given her today for now he would take away wonderful memories of her. But she did not know all of them.

Once, when Julia was standing in the front of the box during a race, she craned her neck to see the start. But she could only distinguish the jockeys in their coloured silk shirts as a bunch of anemones. After the start she could see them as small figures resembling monkeys crouched on the necks of the horses, swaying slightly in a rocking rhythm on the galloping mounts. Paul thrust his glasses into her hand. " Use these," he had urged. " Adjust them here—so." He put his hand over hers to show what he meant. " Focus them on some near object and then adjust to the clearest picture."

His touch at once intimate and direct sent an electric shock through her nerves. She flushed and felt nervous, but when she ventured to turn her head to thank him he seemed engrossed in watching the crowds and had apparently forgotten her. As she glanced at his clear-cut profile she noticed a nervous tic beating under the skin above his jaw, and she guessed that he was as conscious of her as she was of him.

He asked presently, " Enjoying yourself?"

" Oh yes, it is an especially nice day for racing. I'm so glad I could come." The words sounded banal though Julia felt anything but that.

" So am I. But you should be particularly pleased with yourself. Your dress is a success. I hear nothing but praise of you on all sides."

" That is new to me."

" The dress or the praise?"

" Both," and then she added, " I have you to thank for it all."

" Don't, I have done so little for you. I am only too happy you were able to join us." To counter that formality which made him sound pompous, he suggested, " Shall we go down to the paddock again for the next race, or are you too tired?"

" Not a bit. I'd love to go."

As they passed the girl who had sat beside Paul in the car from Paris, she remarked spitefully to her escort, " I do so wish that girl wouldn't hang on to Paul as though she owns him. She has made herself too conspicuous all day. Who is she?"

" That is Paul's latest secretary. She . . ." They had passed out of earshot, and Paul ventured to glance at Julia. She had flushed a little and he knew she must have understood the gist of the remark.

Julia felt rather than saw his look. She turned her head

swiftly to say to him, " Do you think I am hanging on to you, monsieur?"

" No, it is I who am hanging on to you. Anyway, you make a charming pendant. I do not worry, so surely you need not. Don't take any notice of her."

" She is the girl you are seeing in Canada?"

" I expect so." He spoke indifferently. " Her father has a hunting lodge in the Adirondacks. I've been there before."

Julia made no reply. What could she say with truth unless it was, " I'd love to scratch her eyes out." That of course would never do.

Near the paddock, where everyone passes by at some time or other during the afternoon Paul thought he saw Andrew Lester and it occurred to him, " What is that fellow doing here?"

It was annoying to find Julia Brown's cousin across his path. It was on the tip of Paul's tongue to ask Julia if she had expected to see her cousin here, but she was looking in the opposite direction and had not seen Lester, and he did not want to remind her of him.

The brim of her hat was transparent and though he could see the turn of her head he was not certain what she saw unless he bent down and peeped down her hat brim.

Then a strange small thing happened which put Andrew Lester out of his thoughts. As Paul gazed at her profile through the transparent brim he observed the sun glinting through the rose-coloured net yoke of her dress, and her skin glowing beneath.

He felt his emotions risings. At the same time that longing to take care of her, to have her for his own, came over him. It made him feel humble and protective. He thought, Everything has been wrong between us, but I can make it right. When I come back— He touched her arm tentatively to draw her attention, and she turned instantly to hear what he had to say.

" Shall we go back to the box?"

" Oh no, let's watch this parade first. There'll be plenty

of time to see the race if we hurry back after the jockeys have mounted."

She was excited and did not want to miss any of the fun, otherwise she must have observed that Paul's manner was urgent.

" Supposing I want to go back?" he asked half-humorously, half-angry at her refusal to do what he wished, yet half-moved to laugh because this was the first time she had ever said what she really wanted.

" Then of course we'll go," she told him at once. " Do you want to go, monsieur?"

He shook his head, looking down at her upturned face smilingly. " Just as *you* please today."

He glanced nervously about him hoping that Lester was not watching them from some nearby vantage point.

As the mounted horses were led from the paddock Paul and Julia turned to retrace their steps.

Just before the last race Paul missed Julia. He had gone to the front of the box to talk with friends. He thought Julia was behind him in the little salon where they could retire if the weather turned chilly or it rained. There was no protection if the wind came from the wrong direction with rain. They had lunched in the salon. The glass doors were folded back between the room and the box. There was nowhere for Julia to hide. She could be spotted easily.

She was not among the people enjoying Paul's liberal hospitality. Paul thought she had gone to titivate before the journey back to Paris. But when, five minutes later, he turned his head to look for Julia, she was still not there. Abruptly excusing himself he went into the salon to find her. He looked along the gallery that connected the boxes. There was no sign of her.

His first reaction was annoyance for he knew that Julia was unused to the close stare of the crowds. It was something she shrank from. If she went, why did she go? Then he thought of her going with relation to himself. The query made him suddenly suspicious and a sense of uneasiness came over him. If she has gone down to the paddock she must have seen Lester. They are somewhere together, probably talking his business and plotting against me. I don't trust him. And there came another thought, I don't trust her either. From that point Paul's thoughts were a little wild.

With an awful feeling of dread and presentiment that something was wrong, Paul dashed down the staircase. At the bottom he bumped into Georgette, and asked her bluntly, " Have you seen Julia Brown? "

Georgette shrugged, raised her eyebrows delicately and made a little moué. Miss Brown was not a girl who remained in her thoughts unless she was with Paul. Away from Paul she was a girl of no importance. Then she remembered something that would hurt Paul and pay him out for neglecting her all the afternoon. " Oh, yes. I saw her sitting at a café."

" Not my Miss Brown."

" I could not mistake her dress."

" Then she was not alone? "

" No, apparently with a friend, a man not of our party. They were talking earnestly."

Paul's secret fears were realised and his eyes darkened. " Which café? " he snapped.

" I do not know the name. It is on the way to the paddock."

She gasped. Without ceremony Paul who was usually so courteous had gone, and Georgette was left talking to the air.

D

Chapter Seven

MEANWHILE, JULIA had gone to the powder room and opening her bag to take out her compact found that it was missing. She paused to think and decided that it must have fallen out of her bag when she was in the paddock with Paul. It was the last time she had opened the bag. Someone might have picked it up and returned it to the lost property office.

She was twenty minutes ahead of Paul. After inquiries in the paddock she was directed to the lost property office, and disappointed, was on her way back to the enclosure, when she paused. Someone had called her name urgently.

"Julia!"

She glanced over her shoulder, and saw to her amazement Andrew blocking her way, a crowd of people swirling about them. She was unaware that people were staring at her with curiosity, a lovely blonde in a gorgeous dress, unescorted in a race crowd! She had no idea that a lone photographer had sprinted after her from the enclosure and was busy photographing both Julia and Andrew.

"Andrew!" she cried in bewilderment. "What on earth are you doing here?"

He looked grey and ill and for a moment she felt a fleeting compassion for him, even chiding herself for having enjoyed herself without a thought to spare for him.

"I came to find you. I phoned you at his apartment but they said you had come here for the day, and as I had to see you at once I followed you. It was quite simple except that I couldn't waste time dressing for the part."

"But why must you see me so urgently?" she asked, then realised the truth, and her heart which had felt so light and happy, sank like lead in her breast.

All at once she became aware that they were the centre of a group of curious people who were listening to what they were saying and she said nervously, "Let's get out of this and find somewhere quiet to talk."

Andrew looked about him. He saw a café. "We can sit there and talk," he said and his voice had that urgent frightening note that had been there when he first uttered her name.

Julia said quickly, "It's as good as any place, better than standing here anyway. I mustn't be long as I shall be missed, and there will be trouble."

They hurried into the café but it was full and they were just going away when a couple left one of the small tables on the terrace and Julia said, "We must take that. We have no choice." But she did not like the table for though it commanded a good view of the crowds, they were also the cynosure of all eyes. They sat down, ordered some drinks and Julia said at once, "Now what is the matter, Andrew?"

"I heard Roth is off to Canada tomorrow, and I must fix up something about our affairs before he goes." He spoke rather breathlessly knowing that he was pressed for time and they might be interrupted by Paul himself at any moment.

"Why is it so imperative for you to see him?" But she knew already from what Andrew had often hinted at, from what Paul had said and what her own intuition told her.

"To urge him, to beg, even to implore him to give us a break. It is our last chance. By the time he comes back our shares will have flopped. It'll be a walk-over for him, if he thinks the game is worth following up then."

"I never realised it was so bad as this, Andrew."

"I've tried to tell you, but you never seemed able to take it in that we are sinking."

Julia agreed. "I know you did, but honestly, I couldn't imagine such a situation."

It came to her then that her mind had been so full of Paul that she was incapable of taking in outside affairs. Her emotions had swamped all other thoughts and feelings. She had not felt affected by the misfortune of those people who had once been so kind to her, and who now seemed to belong to another world. She was full of remorse. She fell silent. All at once she felt terribly tired, her head and feet ached, and all the lovely emotions that had buoyed her up throughout the day, exciting untold wild fancies, had grown top heavy and fallen over.

"What can I do?" she heard herself ask in a passionate whisper.

Andrew took a long breath. He said, speaking rapidly, "Time is too short for persuasion or guile. You've got to put a straightforward question to him. The answer must be a definite yes or no. If yes then you must see that he acts at once."

"It certainly is serious," she said in a low tone.

His eyes held hers, and the expression in his was tragic. "I'm afraid that everything about this sorry business is underlined." Then he added reflectively, yet with a note of despair that was not lost on her, "Perhaps all this dilly-dallying in the matter, this holding back, this pretence of waiting for opinion and advice from the accountants, bankers and lawyers is part of a plan to corner us when of course he can make any terms he wants."

Julia would not have this. " Monsieur would never play such a mean trick on me," she cried earnestly.

" Not to you, to us—our firm, quite a different matter. He'd call it business anyway. I certainly think he would. But there is a chance that with you mixed up in it, the sex question, you know, odd things could happen, even a miracle. It is a forlorn hope, but it could happen."

It was obvious that Andrew *did* hope and that he relied solely on Julia's efforts now.

She said at once, " Then I will approach Monsieur before he leaves Paris. There is of course the chance that he may leave here and go off with some of his guests in which case he won't return to the apartment until the early hours of tomorrow morning. But he's got to come back if only to get his briefcase, something inseparable with him on these journeys abroad. He leaves Orly Airport at dawn. If I have to sit up all night waiting for him I promise to have this matter out with him. He must have thought about it one way or another."

She saw that her words relieved Andrew of some of his terrible burden. It was touching, the faith he had in her powers. Only Julia knew what little power she had over Monsieur, but she dared not tell Andrew for fear of sapping his confidence in her and depressing him further.

" Oh, Julia, I am relieved. I've been in hell all day searching for you, sometimes catching a glimpse of you but never alone, always with him, and wondering what on earth to do to get you alone. It has been a maddening experience."

She put her hand over his, and all her soul was in her eyes as she comforted. " Dear Andrew. Try not to worry. I'll get in touch with you at seven in the morning. Monsieur has many faults I know, but I have always found him fair."

Andrew looked at her doubtfully. " I hope you are right,"

he told her, repeating the words as though anxious to re-assure himself.

Then, anxious to be doing something, Julia rose hurriedly. " I'd better go back. If Monsieur has missed me and looks for me he will spot me here quickly. He will be too angry to want to help us. I believe he is jealous of you, Andrew. He sometimes acts like it."

" Jealous! There's no need. Surely you've told him so?"

" We know it is silly, but *he* doesn't."

" Does he want you for himself?"

She flushed. " No, but he can't bear to share even his employees."

" I know the sort—they want people's body and soul. Okay, you'd better go. There's the starting bell for the last race. In a few minutes the crowds will be rushing madly for the exits. Hurry back to the enclosure, Julia."

She had wanted to savour the enjoyment of the day, but that was at an end now that she had heard Andrew's troubles.

She ran most of the way, reaching the enclosure just as Paul came up.

" Where have you been?" he demanded harshly. " I thought you were lost and went to look for you."

She had given him a fright, but now that he had found her, the reaction made him angry.

" I'm sorry, monsieur, but I discovered I had lost my powder compact and went to the paddock to look for it," she told him breathlessly.

" In that crowd! Are you crazy? Of course you did not find it?"

" No, someone must have picked it up."

" I could have told you that." He glanced around him, and saw the crowd was already on the move.

" There is no object in joining the others who are probably waiting for us in the car park. Better go there with me now."

Julia sat in the back of the car on the homeward journey. She was tired and shaken, and spoke little. If asked how she felt Julia might have replied, " Like flat champagne." There was no sparkle in her. She was turning over in her mind how to approach Monsieur for Andrew. Once, when held up in a traffic jam, Paul, wondering at her quietness, half-turned in his seat to look back at her. She was sitting demurely with her hands crossed in her lap, her face white and weary, and her big shadowed eyes staring fixedly at some point ahead of the car. It did not require much imagination on Paul's part to realise that Julia's thoughts were far away. The present did not exist for her. It came to him what a small part he had in her life.

Paul stopped at the great black doors of Georgette's family's hotel. It was an impressive building.

" You will join us for dinner, Paul?" she invited, pointedly leaving Julia out.

" Thank you, I shall be delighted," was the formal reply. He chanced to look at Julia as he spoke.

She had heard the invitation and his answer with dismay. Instinctively her hand went out towards him in an appealing gesture, then almost at once fell back in her lap, and a queer haunted look came into her eyes, so that oddly Paul was reminded of some animal at bay.

Without pausing he said smoothly to Georgette, " On second thoughts please excuse me for I recall that there is much to do at the apartment before I leave. I shall look forward to seeing you all in Canada."

When they reached home Paul surprised Julia by saying, " You had better rest now. I am out for dinner."

Julia hesitated on the pavement. " You are coming in before you go?" she asked quickly.

Paul half-smiled. " Have I not said so?"

" Yes, but—" she paused, not knowing how to go on.

" Well?"

" Nothing, only I should like to speak to you before you go."

Paul laughed. His eyes were kind and indulgent. "Ah! I thought you had something on your mind. Go and rest and get out of those fancy clothes. You will feel more natural."

Julia went in slowly, not sure whether Paul would turn up early enough to spare time for her. She dared not push him further, or make a definite appointment. Monsieur hated being pinned down, and at all costs she must not let him get out of temper.

Paul watched her go, a curious look in his fine eyes. *Pauvre chérie*, he thought whimsically, I do believe she is as frightened of me as I am of her—in our different ways.

He was home in less than two hours, and found Julia had taken his advice and was rested. She had changed from the grand rose dress to a simple cotton summer shift and looked young, defenceless and appealing. He was in mellow mood, and longed to see her more cheerful.

He mixed a drink which he poured into two glasses. He offered her a cigarette, lighted it for her, and pulled forward the most comfortable chair in the room for her to rest in, then sat down facing her. It was still light outside. The windows were open to the summer twilight, but the lamps were lighted and gave an air of gaiety to the sombre room.

"Now relax and tell me all about it," he said genially. Then he sank back in his chair, a cigarette in one hand and his glass on the table at his elbow, and looking across at Julia, waited for her to speak. She did not find this easy. Her flow of thought had dried up.

"You seem to be a long time beginning this urgent talk," he chided gently. It was a reminder that he was a busy man, and she was forced to say something to hold his attention.

She raised limpid eyes to his face. "I don't know how to begin." Secretly she began to pray wildly for guidance in the right use of words. To her astonishment Paul said,

"Shall I make a guess?"

She stared at him in astonishment. "You couldn't," she told him flatly.

" I am not blind. Perhaps I see more than you think."

" But—"

" Is it about the Lester take-over?" His voice, she thought, had stiffened.

After a little silence she said, " Yes," and wished that this talk were over.

" Andrew Lester has been pressing you to urge me to buy control of your family's company, the engineering group that has lately been doing so badly?"

Julia felt sick at Monsieur's penetration. She added hesitantly, " There has been a sharp drop lately due to accumulated tax losses. They want an outsider to step in and try to recover values. They think you are the best man. The only man."

Paul looked at her closely. " Your words or your cousin's?" he queried sharply.

" Andrew's," she admitted reluctantly.

" Is he the former manager who wishes to buy up one side of the business?"

" No, Andrew has no spare cash." She spoke in a stronger voice, feeling that Monsieur was an ally, and she must answer his questions as clearly as she could, or they would get nowhere.

There was a long silence, then Paul said, " I do not like taking over any business at the stage your family's business has reached now, when the investment status is poor, though I think in this case there is considerable potential. But I cannot discuss the matter with you. Firstly, I never do business through or with a woman. Secondly you certainly do not understand the intricacies. You are only a mouthpiece, and I resent your interference. You are simply a pawn they are using hoping to influence me to do something I know is unbusinesslike, and against my judgment. There has, too, been unnecessary delay because facts and figures have not been made readily available to the negotiators on my side. They have only themselves to blame for that."

Julia had never seen Paul's face so set and hard. Gone was the bonhomie of earlier in the day when they had met as equals at Chantilly. He would be implacable like this at a boardroom table. She flashed, " You are hard," then remembered that she must not allow her personal feelings to override her tact. Trying to hurt him with barbs would do her cause no good. Recriminations would get her nowhere.

" We are talking business not personalities," he reminded her sharply.

" I am reminded that you have never liked my cousin, and now you have it in your power to help or not, you seem glad to refuse to help. I am sorry I asked you."

Paul waved that aside. " You didn't. I guessed. It was almost too easy. You forget I know why Andrew Lester is in Paris. I am also aware that he confides too much business to you. It is not fair to you."

He shot a question at her and his voice had an edge to it that caused her to shiver. " When did you last see your cousin?"

" I am not going to answer that question," Julia said, recalling that Andrew's last words were, " For heaven's sake don't tell him we have met and discussed this matter, or we'll both be sunk."

" It must have been recently. Your cousin is worried because I am leaving Paris, and any unfinished business will be held over until my return."

Julia compressed her lips to shut in a sharp retort.

Paul went on, " I do not pretend to like your cousin. I certainly deplore his business methods. I am not inclined to help him. For why should I? If only because he is your friend I will not discuss business with you. All this goes deep—deeper than you realise, Miss Brown."

There, it was out now. Paul admitted his jealousy, for that is what it was.

Julia sat up stiffly. Her relaxed feeling went and a certain tension took its place. Her unhappiness at returning empty-

handed to Andrew was so intense that she wanted to cry,
yet she must not do so in front of this man. She caught her
underlip in her teeth to hide its trembling. Then gathering
up all her strength she put down the glass she had been
holding and rose to her feet saying unsteadily, " Then there
is nothing more to be said, monsieur. My apologies for
taking up so much of your valuable time." Her voice grew
stronger and she continued, " I do not know if you have had
many setbacks in business. I should not like my worst enemy
to go through the trials my uncle and cousin are undergoing
now. They have given me the only love and kindness I have
had for many years, and for that reason, when they are in
trouble, as now, knowing that I am employed by you and
have, so to speak, your ear, they asked me to intercede for
them. As it has turned out I have failed, for there is nothing
I should have liked better than to give them some small return for all that they have done for me. That is why I was
willing to approach you."

Paul was silent when she finished, his eyes fixed on her
face. When he spoke at length his voice was gruff :

" You are not talking business now. You are appealing
to me as a man and making some impression. But don't you
realise that I cannot use other people's money entrusted to
me for wrongful purposes or wildcat schemes? But I can
use my own money as I like. I can write out a cheque to
cover their temporary difficulties. It might even be a gift,
but it is with my money."

" They do not want your charity, but the practical help
that only your brains can give their Company."

Paul passed that over. He continued inexorably,

" I am willing to tide them over, at least until I return.
I will do so if you can answer me one question satisfactorily."

Julia lifted her chin. The gesture steadied her. " What is
it?"

" Did you see Andrew Lester at the races today?"

Julia's face clouded. She had no idea what to say. She

longed to tell Paul the truth, but she was afraid. " Supposing I did, what then?" she cried defiantly, but anguish at her lie rushed through her, and she flushed rosily.

Paul's mouth was grim. " Then so far as I am concerned the merger is closed."

" And if I did not?"

" Then I shall give you a covering cheque to send to your uncle in London."

" You are making a personal thing of this," she accused passionately.

" I am."

That decided Julia. She said deliberately, " No, I did not see Andrew today. How could I when I was with you most of the time?" Her passion had died suddenly and she felt stone cold.

" Yet he was at Chantilly."

She started uneasily, and looked hard at him as though she would read his thoughts.

" Did you see him?" Her thoughts were chaotic, yet she must take a chance.

" I thought I did." That word ' thought ' gave her such sudden relief that she felt sick.

Almost without pause she seized upon Paul's indecision, and she said in a calmer tone, " If my cousin had been there he would have brought himself to my notice." Again she was nauseated because disaster had been averted by a miracle.

Paul, too, was relieved. It did not occur to him to doubt Julia's word. He had always found her truthful. She was distressed and overwrought by his close questioning, but that was understandable. He realised from past experience in money dealings with her that she was a girl who would dislike intensely having to ask any man's help in trouble. He had no doubt that she had been jockeyed into this by her people. He was able to feel sorry for her now that his mind was reassured about her cousin and was even anxious to soothe her.

He said, " Give me your glass. Your drink must be warm and mawkish. I shall mix you another drink."

He rose and took the glass from her. In doing so their fingers touched.

Hers was cold, and he exclaimed sharply.

Paul put down the glass quickly and turning, took her hand in both of his saying, " You are trembling. Your hands are icy." He chafed first one hand and then the other striving to warm them. " There is no need for you to be afraid of me," he told her gently, and his voice brought a lump to her throat and an unruly stinging sensation behind her eyes. Julia made no reply.

Paul opened his fingers and looked down at her hand lying limply on his palm, looking like a crushed lily, and he said, " poor hand—so white and fragile! This wretched talk with me must have spoilt your day." Then he asked a question which had occurred to him earlier. " What happened to make you quiet so suddenly this afternoon? You were bright as a bird at *déjeuner*."

" I don't know, unless it was that I had not fully understood the implications of your going to Canada until Mademoiselle Georgette spoke of your visiting her family in Canada. I knew that while you were away for a month nothing could be done for my uncle until you returned."

" I see," he said, nodding in answer to some unspoken query in his mind. He let go her hand and went to the table to mix a fresh drink. While his back was towards her Julia repaired the ravages anger had caused to her face. When he gave her the glass she was reasonably calm again.

" Try this, but don't nurse it too long or that will have to be thrown away, too."

" Such a waste! "

" I was not thinking of that but of the good a potent drink will do you."

Presently Paul went over to her desk, and sitting down at it wrote a large cheque which he slipped into an envelope and fastened up. " Send this to your uncle," he said. " Tell him that I will deal with this matter immediately on my return."

He spoke in his usual businesslike tone. He put the envelope in her lap. " You win," he said, and took away her empty glass.

Julia looked down. She bit her lips to still their trembling. The lump in her throat refused to be swallowed. She could not see the envelope for her eyes were overflowing with tears. She could not hide them. They rained down her cheeks on to her hands which were folded in her lap.

There was a short silence, then Paul cried in consternation, " *Bon dieu*, what is the matter now?"

She half-raised her hands in a supplicating gesture, then let them fall again.

" Please do not look at me. I shall be all right in a moment. I am so very sorry to cry like this, but—it is such a relief."

She dug her closed fists into her eyes, struggling to master her emotion and regain self-control. But it was not only relief that brought the flood of tears. It was shame because she had deceived Monsieur. She longed to tell him the truth and throw herself on his mercy, but it was too late. The mischief was done.

Paul did not speak. He leant over the back of her chair, put his hand on her head and slightly ruffled her hair. It was meant to be a comforting gesture.

Then he said quietly, " Cry away. It had to come anyway. You have been so tensed up. I will leave you alone for a few minutes."

She heard the door shut. It was a relief to be alone for a little while, and Julia made several great efforts to force back her sobs.

When Paul returned she was calm again though her eyes were swollen and pink. He said briskly, " Now what about another drink?"

" No more, thank you. I've had enough." Her voice was

thick but she looked at him as he spoke, and they smiled with understanding at each other.

They spoke of many things for a long while. Paul brought out his briefcase and gave Julia last minute directions about his mail, and then he said, " I think I have covered everything. Oh, one thing more, nothing to do with business—" He took a deep breath before he spoke which caught her attention. Could it be that Monsieur was shy of asking her something?

" You will remain in this flat while I am in Canada?"

Julia was surprised. " That has already been arranged, Monsieur."

" Yes, but I must be sure that you will not be weak and permit yourself to be tempted to run away, perhaps for a short while."

" Oh no. I have nowhere to go. Besides who would want to tempt me?"

" I do not know, but remember Marie and Gaston have charge of you." Then he laughed shortly with relief. " *Bon.* I have now your assurance that you will be here to welcome me on my return?"

" Of course, monsieur."

" Then I am content. It is not for long—four weeks. You will find repose from me and see me in a different perspective. I am not the ogre people believe me to be. I am human underneath."

It was only afterwards, when Paul was flying to Canada that Julia remembered she had not thanked him for the cheque. What would he think of her?

She heard Paul leave the apartment at dawn. He spoke to Gaston in a muted tone though she could not distinguish what he said. Lying in the darkness she thought of him with love and longing, wishing it was her luck to go with him, wondering what on earth she was going to do through the long days without him. How she would miss that curt, " Take a note please, Miss Brown."

That chapter was over for the time being, anyhow. When

the door was shut she turned over in bed and burying her face in the pillow sobbed as though her heart would break, not for Paul but for self-pity because she could not have his love.

When Julia rang up Andrew in the morning as promised he took her to task querulously for being five minutes late.

"Don't you realise I've been lying awake all night wondering if you failed to move him, imagining God knows what? It's been hell."

"I'm sorry, Andrew. I had a bad night, too, then overslept," she excused herself meekly.

Andrew did not comment. He asked quickly, "Is Roth going to help?"

"I think he will. He has given me a cheque to post to uncle. I am to tell him not to worry, that Monsieur will give the matter further attention when he comes back in a month's time."

"How much is the cheque for?"

"I do not know. He gave it to me in a sealed envelope."

"It may be a small one? In that case he might have saved himself the trouble of signing it."

"I don't think so."

"Well, I shall soon know. In the meantime I'll call for the envelope with the cheque in it and take it to London."

"I have special instructions to post it myself," she told him firmly.

"Nonsense! Give it to me. He will never know how it gets there."

"I am going to post it now. And Andrew——?"

"Yes?" He spoke with scarcely concealed impatience.

"You must not call at this apartment—ever."

"Why not? Are those *his* orders?"

"He—well, yes."

"Cheek! But he never liked me."

Julia laughed. "You don't like him either."

"Because he is so stinkingly rich."

" He works very hard for those riches."

" Are you taking his part against me?"

" Well, you are being rather silly, especially as he has been so generous to Uncle."

" We'll see about that. In the meantime I shall not be calling at the apartment because I am going to London. I shall be back in Paris by the time Roth returns. Someone will have to keep him to his word. If you've gone over to his side it will be of no use counting on you."

" He won't need prodding. He remembers even the smallest thing," she said proudly.

Chapter Eight

WITH PAUL'S going abroad it was as though an iron curtain had descended between him and Julia. Her only connection with him was the mail, and these were collected by a commissionaire from the main office twice a week.

Julia grew thin with the ache of longing for him that soon became a physical pain. From having too much to do she now had too little. She worked harder at her French, and went out for long walks, or took to shop-window gazing. She went sightseeing in parties arranged by Cook's. She made excursions with tourists to ancient and monumental Paris. But she knew nothing of the Paris of the Gourmet, or Fashionable Paris, the Paris of Society, or what Andrew had once called " Gay Paree "—all a part of Parisian life to be savoured in company with a man who knew his way around.

On some of her trips with tourists Julia spoke to many people, but there it ended. They were birds of passage only.

The evenings were longest for then her heart was loneliest. She thought of Paul then. There was no need for her to find out the truth about her feelings towards him. Love had been growing in her heart for him from the beginning. There would never be another man for her except Paul.

Anguish came over her when she pondered how to awaken love for herself in his heart. She knew that there was another woman in Paul's life, who had created so much damage in him against others. She had once heard one of Paul's friends say, "Who would look at another girl after knowing Chantal?" Julia had once seen a photograph of Chantal, and it bore out what this man said. Paul had opened his wallet and the photograph had slipped out and fallen on to the carpet. Paul had retrieved it at once, but Julia's eyes had been focused on the snap and guessed whose image he was treasuring. As people had said, Chantal was beautiful. Julia told herself in desperation that she was willing to fight against someone in possession of Paul's heart; but how did one fight?

At last the four weeks were up. Julia went almost wild with joy that last day and bought masses of flowers for the salon, making it look very gay and welcoming, uncaring in her own joy at his homecoming what Monsieur would say at this flower-decked room.

Neither Gaston nor Marie knew the exact moment when he would arrive. "We never know," they told her as they cleaned and polished the apartment.

Julia was sick with excitement and could not touch her *petit-déjeuner*. She went to the hairdresser's. All that day she was either up in the heights of joy, or down wretchedly in despair. Her spirits alternated between the two throughout the day.

Evening came, but still there was no sign of Paul. Julia did not reach the dizzy heights of joy after dark. Instead

she wallowed at the lowest ebb of despair. A commissionaire
created a false alarm when he brought in late a case of
papers from the main office. Julia took them from the case,
neat cardboard blue covers containing business matters tied
with pink tape.

With something of a shock the saw the name—Andrew
Lester Ltd., together with the names of two other firms
in which she knew he was interested.

Her heart leapt as she realised that Monsieur had kept
his word, to get down to this special business on his return.
Her uncle had written acknowledging the safe arrival of the
cheque and looking forward to negotiating a successful
business deal with Paul, but it had been a guarded letter and
clearly he was afraid of saying too much.

Julia longed to untie the pink tape and read the notes on
her uncle's business, but she knew that Monsieur would be
angry if she did. Nothing must mar Paul's homecoming. She
counted so much on the frail hope that Paul also would find
time to do a little heart searching while he was away.

Three days later Monsieur arrived unexpectedly, in one
of those rare moments when Julia was not thinking of him.

She was sitting curled up in a deep comfortable chaise
longue, banked with soft cushions making notes of a tour
she was taking the following day at Versailles, for she had
thought in desperation, I can't stand this uncertainty any
longer, when Paul arrived home unexpectedly, without ringing the bell. The first Julia knew of his coming was when,
hearing a sound she looked up and saw the door open and
Paul standing on the threshold looking wonderfully fit.

" Mademoiselle! " He bowed slightly, and she saw that
he was smiling at her.

She jumped to her feet. " Monsieur! " There was no mis-
taking the surprise and gladness in her voice. Throwing
aside her notebook and pencil, Versailles forgotten, she went
towards him swiftly her hand outstretched in greeting. " We
expected you days ago, and have been on tenterhooks ever
since, wondering what can have happened to you."

" Surely not? I sent a message saying that I was prolonging my stay for an extra holiday." He took her hand in his, pressed it gently then let it go.

" No message came here."

" We must inquire into that, for I sent it personally. How are you?"

Banal words, yet somehow anything between these two seemed so important. Julia, in welcoming and receptive mood, her disappointment of the last few days over, read deeper meanings into Paul's polite phrases than was meant, if only because she wanted Paul to feel concerned about her well-being.

" I am very well, thank you. And you?"

" I, too, am very well."

" Did you have an enjoyable trip, Monsieur?"

" Oh, very. There is a large lake near the house where I spent most of my time, and we sailed and fished when I could spare the days. I found it peaceful and soothing."

" We! " Her heart felt faint and dismayed. So Georgette's companionship was the secret of Paul's fitness and general well-being. The holiday seemed to have taken ten years off his age. He appeared young and boyish. In some ways it made her feel sad, for surely he would realise how much he had to feel thankful to Georgette for. As her face fell and she was quiet for a short while, by comparison Paul was very gay. He did all the talking. He said, " We will dine together, and I shall tell you all about those monster fishes I caught."

He was so happy that she tried hard to imitate him and do nothing to mar the joy of his homecoming. She cried laughingly, " Oh, I've heard those fishermen's stories before."

Paul laughed with her. " Have you, indeed! Well, I promise that if my stories are exaggerated at least they will also be entertaining," he told her. Then he added, " But I forget. I have been away and to eat at home is an appealing novelty. You have probably eaten here every night and would prefer to go out. What do you think?"

"It is for you to say. Why not please yourself, for I do not mind either way." And she thought, Anywhere will do so long at it is with you.

Paul replied at once, "Then I prefer my home. It is new to me, or it seems so after the practical furniture of a log cabin in the backwoods." He looked appreciatively about him. "What lovely flowers! So gay! Are they gifts?" The last words were sharp as a sudden thought struck him, and out of keeping with the fulsome praise of the vases of flowers.

"Yes, I bought them for myself, just for fun. I know you'll think I am extravagant, especially as you do not like flowers."

Paul stared wide-eyed. "Now why do you say that? I love flowers in a salon."

It was Julia's turn to look surprised. "But you said—" she was beginning in perplexity, when Paul remembering, cried, "Oh, my dear Miss Brown, that was long ago—yesterday. This is another day. This evening I can wish for no nicer welcome than the message of these flowers which cheer up the salon and suit you so well."

"Then I am glad I bought them."

By that time Gaston had heard Paul's voice. He came hurrying in to greet him, saying in voluble French, "This is an unexpected pleasure, m'sieu'. We have been waiting for you, but you did not come. M'm'selle was disconsolate. No word. Nothing."

"I sent a cable by telephone from the Adirondacks to my office in Quebec for them to dispatch immediately. My hosts begged me to enter for a fishing contest. I did and I won. I caught the largest fish of the season. It broke my net before I landed it."

Unexpectedly because she was so overjoyed at seeing him and feeling emotional, Julia laughed hysterically. "A fisherman's tall story! For all we know it was a sprat."

Paul caught her humour with his swift Gallic mind. " Perhaps it is a little bit tall," he admitted laughingly, " but not, I assure you, so small as a sprat."

Because they were both happy and laughing Gaston joined in though he had no idea what the joke was about. The little salon had not seemed so light and gay for a long while. When the laughter died down Gaston rubbed his hands and inquired what m'sieu' would like to eat.

Paul replied, " Can Marie cook one of her super surprise dinners?"

" For how many, m'sieu'?"

" For two. Mademoiselle and I are celebrating alone. We shall be drinking champagne." He took a bunch of keys from his pocket, detached one and tossed it over to Gaston. " Get out a couple of bottles of the best vintage. This is an occasion." But he did not say *what* occasion.

Later the two sat at a little flower-decked round table for dinner. Gaston served from a trolley. It was an intimate occasion. Paul talked volubly of his travels and the journey home. Julia had never known him to be so gay and talkative. He seemed ten years younger in looks and spirits.

With a pang she thought, So this is the effect Georgette has on him. He will be announcing his engagement to her before the end of dinner. That is why he asked for vintage wine. And she envied the girl who had so much power over him.

Once, during dinner, Julia felt constrained to say, " You keep saying ' we,' monsieur. Who was your companion on these expeditions?"

" Why Mademoiselle Georgette's family—" and he went on to tell her of a sudden squall that blew up over the lake which caught them unawares, as they were not keeping a proper lookout, and how they were all thrown into the water when the boat capsized.

Julia shuddered. " I wonder you weren't drowned."

" Too many people about for that."

" I should think Mademoiselle Georgette hated getting

wet," she remarked involuntarily and she thought, I bet she
was furious at being nearly drowned! She pictured Georgette immaculately got up for *le sport* of fishing, and what
she must look like with spoilt make-up and wet hair.

Paul stared. " But she was not with us on that occasion.
We were alone," he told her.

In a way that was a worse admission and Julia faltered.
" But you said ' we.' Naturally I thought you meant you and
Mademoiselle Georgette."

" You thought wrong, Miss Brown," Paul replied chuck-
ling at her mistake, and perhaps a little at his own thoughts
for he had not been blind to Julia's obvious interest in and
jealousy of Georgette. " In this case the ' we,' were
Mademoiselle's younger sister, Charmian and her brother
Henri—"

" Oh!" Julia longed to ask how old Charmian was, but
Paul supplied the answer to her unspoken question. He
laughed wickedly as though he read her thoughts, saying,
" Charmian is a sweet *poupée* of fifteen who already knows
all the questions and answers much better than her elder
sister, and certainly much better than I do, while Henri,
younger still, has all the characteristics though not the
appearance of a mischievous monkey. I am not surprised
the boat capsized. They are a careless couple and insuffer-
ably cheeky. Just before it happened I was hoping it would
capsize and they would both be drowned."

Julia tried to look suitably shocked at his sentiments, but
she could not keep it up and began to laugh. " I wish I had
been there."

" So do I. It is a lovely spot, the air from the pinewoods
blown across the lake is like wine, very heady. It could have
been fun, too. I do not think you would have minded falling into the lake, though it was cold, providing of course
that you could swim."

" Yes, I can swim, and I can sail a boat," she replied
eagerly.

" That is news. Who taught you the craft?"

" My cousin, Andrew."

It was a fatal admission. Paul's mood changed at once. Gone was the bonhomie of the last hour, and he said with something of his old intolerance, " Oh, Andrew?" Julia was sorry she had mentioned Andrew. It was clearer than ever that Paul did not like him, for a heavy frown had gathered on his forehead like a black cloud, and it was slow to disperse.

Then he asked almost casually, " Did you see much of your cousin while I was in Canada?"

" No, he went back to England an hour after you flew out from Paris."

" With the envelope containing my cheque?" The words were bitten out from tight lips.

" No, I told him you had charged me to post it."

" So he wanted to take it?"

" Yes, to save time."

" But you posted it?"

" Yes."

" Am I really to believe that?" Paul asked after a pause during which his eyes searched her face for the truth.

Julia looked back at him startled. " It is the truth, monsieur."

" *Bien*, let it pass," he said almost indifferently.

" No, you are not being fair. I did obey your orders and post the letter to my uncle."

" *Bien*. I will accept that. I should never have questioned your word only once you were not truthful with me. And if once why not other times? You cannot blame me for the difficulty I find in guessing what you mean." He paused, and looked across at her seriously. " Well?"

Julia was about to disclaim the base insinuation. She had forgotten the occasion to which Paul referred. Then she remembered clearly that she had lied to Paul about meeting Andrew at Chantilly races. What had he found out? How much did he really know of the events of that day? As he appeared to be waiting for her to say something, she admitted quietly. " Yes, I do recall telling you a deliberate lie, monsieur."

Paul drew in a quick breath. " Was it the time when you said you had not seen your cousin on the racecourse at Chantilly in June?"

" Yes, monsieur. I am very sorry."

" Perhaps you hoped I would not find out?"

" How did you?"

In answer Paul took out his wallet, and opening it with maddening deliberateness, took out a page cut from a glossy magazine. He handed it silently to her.

Julia took it wonderingly and looked at it. She saw herself sitting close to Andrew at a little round-topped café table, an elegantly dressed girl and Andrew, who had been so upset by money worries he had not even bothered to dress suitably for the races. The photograph had caught them at a moment, when Andrew had been in tears, terribly distraught by the position of the company he managed, and she was full of pity for him. His hand was on the table, and hers rested on it, trying to comfort him.

" You did not think the photographer had taken that photograph?" Paul asked harshly.

She shook her head. " I was too disturbed myself to bother about outsiders."

" Touching, is it not?"

" You must put what interpretation you please on it, monsieur."

" What anyone would think."

" Perhaps. I suppose some busybody sent it to you?"

" Yes, one of the friends we were with that day."

" It was a mean trick."

Paul let that pass. " It is you though?" he said, still in that hard tone.

" Oh, yes. I can't deny that."

" Then I will tear it up. If I had not shown it to you you would never have believed me."

" No."

Paul tore the sheet across several times, and threw the pieces into the wastepaper basket. " Was it an arranged meeting?"

" I had no idea that Andrew would be there."

" I suppose you are sorry I found out?"

" Yes. I am sorry, too, that I lied."

" Why did you?"

" I was so afraid you would refuse to help. I had a headache and I was desperate."

" Do you mean you were afraid of my anger, or me?" he asked wonderingly.

" Yes."

" I must have seemed like a monster to you in those days."

" Oh no, monsieur. But you did not like Andrew."

She was astonished at the violence of his expression when he said, " I do *not* like your cousin. I cannot bear that you should be seen out with him. I hate his influence over you."

" I have never been influenced by Andrew."

" There I beg to differ."

Julia was silent. The glow of that lovely feeling which had come over her at sight of him, of having him safely home again, of finding him gentle, tender and sweet, was fading fast. Already the polish had worn off. Monsieur had not really changed at all. He had been nursing a grudge against her in the shape of that telltale page from a glossy magazine. It was only her silliness that had imagined he was different, that parting had made him softer.

" You have nothing more to say?" How final the words were. Perhaps he was going to give her the sack. She knew he had a hatred of untruthfulness. She waited for the blow to fall and even wondered how she could take it.

" No. I've said I am sorry."

Paul replied, " Then this matter is closed for ever, but please do not do this ever again. I simply cannot take it from you."

Her lashes were wet as she smiled at him through a veil of tears.

Then Paul asked, "What were you so busy doing when I came in?" She knew by the tone that he had observed in that first glance he was waiting and really wanted to hear.

After a moment during which Julia steadied herself she was able to tell him. "Only the times the coach starts tomorrow on a day trip to Versailles."

"*Dieu*! Is that how you have found amusement this last month?"

"These conducted daily tours are a good way for people like me to see Paris. I rather like going for there is always someone willing to talk to me."

"I bet there is."

"Not men. I mean girls."

"You must have been lonely, yes? I had not thought of that."

"Rather. If you have observed, though why should you, I like people around me."

Paul picked up the notebook from the chaise-longue where she had thrown it down when he came in. He studied it for a while in silence, then tossed it aside.

"I have never been on one of these jaunts myself. Perhaps I have missed something. They give comprehensive details of many tours. One of these days—but there, of what use? I am a busy man in Paris. Work has accumulated in my absence and I face a mountain of work in the next few weeks. I have had my holiday."

Then Paul applied himself to being a good host. "Is that meal the way you like it? French cooking is not always to the English taste."

"It is delicious. Marie is a first class cook. She can do no wrong."

"Then we are at fault. We have been talking too earnestly. Your dinner must be cold. Lukewarm meat is like lukewarm drink—unpalatable. I will ring for Gaston to take it away and bring a fresh dish, and this time we shall talk of only pleasant things."

" And hurt Marie's feelings?"

" I am not concerned with her feelings. You are eating this dinner and not Marie, and you must have the best to-night."

That struck home. She was unused to tenderness, and her lips trembled badly.

" Now what have I said wrong?" Paul demanded.

" I am not used to being looked after."

" Then it is time you are."

Paul complimented Julia on her dress and her looks. " You are wonderful tonight. I suppose I took a risk in going away but it had to be."

It was all most exciting to hear but ambiguous, and Julia trembled again with delight this time. What did he mean? She wished he would be more explicit. She longed to ask him but decided not to force anything nice or nasty from him for she was still unsure of herself with him and had no confidence in their friendship.

Chapter Nine

A WEEK later Julia had a letter from her Uncle. He wrote that things were looking up at home. Roth had made a firm offer to take-over their company and the Board had decided to accept.

As a kind of postscript he added that Andrew had fallen in love with a local girl and wanted to get married. " It is a good thing," he wrote. " Marriage will give him incentive, something he badly needs."

Julia decided to tell Paul about Andrew at the first possible moment. Alas, that opportune moment did not arrive for some days, for Paul was in a bad mood and unapproachable. Flowers were banished from the salon. Work was the order of the day. Julia could do nothing right. Yet there was a certain subtle difference in their relationship.

Once, when Paul was dictating a " note " to Julia he paused unaccountably, at a loss for words. She glanced up at him inquiringly, and caught him looking at her, his expression intense. His eyes slid away almost immediately, but not before she had caught the strange look in them. They were highlighted and glistened, as though burning with some inward passion. Julia had never seen him so disturbed.

Almost at once she felt oddly confused. A flush rose in her cheeks and spread even to her neck. What powerful emotion had come over him? There was no time to dwell on the moment or even to analyse it. That might come later, when she had the time to dwell on the look in retrospect.

Paul recovered quickly, and his voice loud and harsh cut through her emotions and brought her back with a jerk to practical things.

The memory persisted for it had brought a glow to her starved heart, the warmth of desire.

Later in the month Charmian and Henri came over to Paris for a short visit. Julia went out for a short walk one morning, leaving the apartment tidy and peaceful as usual. Paul had not yet put in an appearance though she had seen Gaston carry in his *petit-déjeuner* and mail. She saw no one who could warn her that a noisy invasion was imminent.

When she returned half an hour later, shrieks and shouts came from the salon. In astonishment Julia opened the door and saw the havoc made by two spoilt children. They were throwing cushions at Paul who sat at a disadvantage in his usual large chair and let them wreak their mischievous spirits on him. Paul's hair was on end, his arms lunging about, either returning cushions as ammunition, or staving off a combined onslaught to twist his nose. To Julia he looked like a great boy no better-mannered than his visitors.

All three turned flushed faces towards the door, and suddenly the fight was over. It was Paul who spoke first. He struggled to his feet and passed his hand several times over his untidy hair.

" It is Mademoiselle Brown," he told them. But the

children after that first pause of surprise and silence during which they found that Julia was not so much older than themselves refused an introduction.

" Say, it's Julia," they shouted. The girl ran towards her. She was as tall as Julia, but had longer legs. Henri, younger, but more circumspect than his sister, came over to bow and shake hands with her. He asked in good English though coloured with an American accent, " We have heard all about you from Uncle Paul. He told us you are his secretary and live in this apartment. I think," and here he paused, his great black eyes on Julia's face, " that you are pretty enough to be—"

He hesitated and looked slyly at Paul, who interrupted him sternly, " *Attendez! Tenez!* You are to keep that to yourself. I do not wish to hear."

There was something so forbidding about Paul's tone that both children stared at him abashed.

Julia hung her head. She was not slow to guess what Henri had been about to say. As the full meaning of that broken sentence burst upon her she felt dizzy and sick. Then came a sense of shame and humiliation. She could not help glancing at Paul. She guessed that he knew, too. He was not looking at Julia but at Henri, obviously thinking that the boy was too advanced for his age. She could see that he was disturbed and even angry.

Somehow, in the easy way of life during the holidays in the log cabin in the Adirondacks, Henri had seemed younger and more boyish. Paul was surprised to hear such mature ideas coming from the boy who was still some years from college life.

What he needs, Paul thought wrathfully, is a thrashing for speaking so brashly. He could not do this so he said brusquely, " Now you two be off. Wait for me in the vesti-bule downstairs. I have to dictate a ' note ' to Mademoiselle Brown, and I must have quiet to collect my thoughts."

When they had gone, Julia looking quiet and stricken, sat down at her desk and drew her writing pad towards

her. Her hand, holding a pencil, was poised to "take a
note."

Paul went over to her. He took the pencil from her nerve-
less fingers.

"I do not want you to take a note. I said that to get rid
of them. I want to apologise for Henri's stupidity. I am so
sorry his foolish words hurt you."

Julia listened in silence, then she said quietly, "He is
not to be blamed. What would anyone think who knew I
lived in your apartment? Henri is right. We have invited
that sort of criticism." Then she added wonderingly, "But
who could have told Henri's people that I lived here? He
must have overheard someone discussing the position."

Paul did not know how to answer her. Clearly Henri's
informant, whether she was aware of it or not, was his elder
sister Georgette. If Julia had not already tumbled to that
truth she soon would. It would hurt her even more than
she was already.

He repeated in a deep voice, "I am sorry. Once upon a
time, when I was hurt myself I would not have minded
hurting you or anyone. Hurting others seemed to assuage
my own ache. But now all is different. I no longer wish to
hurt others, and certainly I would not have had this happen
to you today for worlds. I assure you that those children
shall not come here again."

"Oh, please, don't stop them. They seem to like you so
much."

"There is no sense in your being hurt further."

"I will try to forget what they said."

Paul could not have been kinder. Towards evening a
florist's girl brought a huge sheaf of roses for Julia. The card
beneath the cellophane bag bore the words, "From Paul."

A week later Paul said to Julia, "I am taking those two
devils out to Versailles tomorrow. Owing to my sudden return from Canada I recall that you had to postpone the
visit you had arranged for yourself. Would you care to join

E

us? I warn you it means you will have to do your share of
looking after them, for they are even wilder than when you
saw them last week—and this is Paris not the backwoods."

Julia jumped at the chance. " I'd love to go. What time
do you want to start?"

" Soon after ten o'clock. Wrap up warm for there is an
east wind blowing and it can be cold in that huge park."

Julia scarcely slept that night. The prospect of being with
Paul all day, with no business between them to annoy him
was too wonderful to miss and she looked forward to going.

It was a fine cold day.

They drove out to Versailles in Paul's car. He was driving
and without being invited Charmian jumped in beside him.
Henri and Julia sat on the back seat.

Charmian was on her best behaviour, and seemed older
than her years in her elder sister's cast-off coat. She had
obviously been tutored by Paul that if she did not behave
she would be pushed into the back seat with Henri. Julia
thought she seemed subdued, and it was pathetic to see the
way she snuggled up to Paul as her friend and protector.

The four lunched at a restaurant overlooking the side of
the great Place D'Armes. They did not go into the Palace,
but visited the Trianons and the little hamlet where Marie-
Antoinette and her ladies used to play at being land girls,
this last place smothered with a kind of nostalgic imagin-
ings which reached out to Julia if not to the others.

The fountains had finished playing for the year. As it was
late autumn there was a scent of decay in the air. Dead
leaves were thick on the ground, though there were the remains of many bonfires, some still smouldering. Henri kicked
up leaves as he walked, but Charmian, in the throes of her
first adoring love, hung on to Paul's arm. She was tired.
Henri, simply because he would not be outdone in hero-
worship would have taken Paul's free arm, but the latter
shook him off.

" Mademoiselle Brown is tired, too. Perhaps she would
like the help of my other arm?"

He looked quizzically sideways at Julia's profile and thought she was fatigued. But Julia shook her head. She dared not take Paul's arm, for he would feel how her hand trembled at the contact, when he would most certainly have guessed that she was feeling as emotional as Charmian.

She paused making an effort to control her voice, then managed to say coolly, " Thank you, but I am not that tired, monsieur."

There was a short silence, and for a moment Julia panicked in case Monsieur took her rebuff wrongly, but he only remarked, " Independent are you not?"

She made no reply. But her face remained pale and there was a look of strain in the eyes that met his momentarily, and he was moved to pity. He suggested, " If you and Charmian will sit on the seat outside the gates, Henri and I will bring the car to you and there will be no need for anyone to walk until they drop."

Charmian obediently sat down by Julia, but she was an unwilling companion and sighed heavily several times.

" What is the matter?" Julia inquired at length, finding the girl's sighs depressing.

" I would rather have gone with Uncle Paul."

" But you are tired. Remember how you clung to his arm because your feet ached?"

" Half of that was pretence. I wanted to *touch* Uncle Paul. I am in love with him, Mademoiselle Brown." And again she sighed oppressively.

Julia longed to smile at the naïveté of the admission, but she managed to keep a straight face.

" The trouble is that Uncle Paul is popular. Everybody is in love with him. Are you not, too?"

" What a quaint girl you are! Fancy asking me such a question! I am beyond the age of having crushes on people. Besides, it would indeed be foolish of me to fall in love with my employer. If I were and he knew it I should get the sack."

" But everyone believes—"

"I don't care what they believe, or what nonsense you have heard," Julia said vigorously. "It just isn't true."

"But you see him each day. If you were in love with him, it would be easy for you to make him fall for you."

Julia looked down. She said, "I doubt that. Nothing to do with Monsieur Roth is easy. I am sure that Monsieur would never permit himself to get involved with such a useful secretary as I am."

"That is what *you* think. But Uncle Paul is very human."

Julia gave a short laugh. "I see him so often possibly I know him almost too well, and that *could* put me off him as much as he could be put off me."

Charmian looked sideways at her in distaste. "The English are too cold," she said. "Love with them is a business, not a lovely passion. You must have a stone in place of a heart, Julia."

Julia laughed. "You are too precocious, Charmian, The best thing you can do is to forget Monsieur. So many girls falling in love with him, and willing to make doormats of themselves tend to spoil him for the girl he will eventually marry."

Julia did not believe a word she said, but the rough advice seemed to appease the torment in her heart. Neither did Charmian understand all that Julia said, for though they spoke in English some of it was beyond Charmian, especially the "doormat."

"It could be me though," the latter said hopefully.

"It could be anyone, for love is not to be bought or had for asking, or begged for, it just happens."

Charmian's expressive face took on a mournful look. "But suppose luck passes me by?"

Julia thought she was going to cry, so she said briskly, "You really must snap out of this mood, Charmian, or you will bore him. If you are not smiling when he drives up Monsieur will think I have been cruel to you."

"So you have," Charmian flashed. "You've tried to put

me off him. You have no sympathy. Even history books call
you ' perfidious Albion,' and they are right."

Julia said no more. She was thankful when Paul drove
up and said, " I had difficulty in getting out of the park.
I seemed hopelessly hemmed in. Now who is going to sit
beside me on the way back? Charmian has had her turn.
Shall we invite Mademoiselle Brown to fill the place of
honour?"

Charmian's face fell. She had smiled obediently as they
drove up, Henri sitting beside Paul. When Henri got out to
open the back door she prepared to slip into his place. Now
her pretty lips pouted. " Julia doesn't want to," she said
quickly, " but I do."

" What *are* you talking about?"

" I am in love with you, Uncle Paul, but Julia isn't, and
so the back seat will be more comfortable."

" Ah, and how do you know that?" Paul asked blandly,
but his frown indicated annoyance.

" Because she said so—just now."

" Then she is being cruel to me, and I thought she had
such a kind face," Paul mocked lightly.

At a sign from Julia, Henri opened the rear door. Julia
got in and sat behind Paul. " I wish you wouldn't talk such
a lot of nonsense, Charmian," she cried pettishly.

Unexpectedly Paul interrupted, " It is nonsense that
amuses me. I hope Charmian tells me more of this love
disease or business or whatever it is that has attacked her.
I shall be most interested in what she has to say. Get in,
Charmian, but the condition of sitting by me is that you
amuse me."

Julia leant forward. She was afraid of what the indiscreet
Charmian might tell Paul. " Please, Monsieur! " she begged.

Her warm breath tickled his ear. She was so close to him
that Paul knew if he turned his head he could kiss her. He
laughed wickedly. " That is prettily said, but I do feel the
need of amusement."

Charmian snuggled up to him like a cat seeking warmth.

Julia sat back and tried to relax. Her attitude was fatalistic. Henri got in beside her and chattered inexhaustibly about nothing, unaware of his listener's reactions.

Scraps of talk floated back to Julia from the front seat occupants, for Charmian's high-pitched young voice was penetrating. Julia's ears burned when she heard Charmian repeating some of the conversation that had taken place between them on the bench outside the gates. Once she heard Monsieur's deep laugh.

The truth is, she thought, I talk too much. Charmian is too receptive. Then she thought recklessly, But why should I care what she says? It won't make any difference to me now. If it had not been for Chantal I might have had a chance. I came too late on the scene. They were bitter-sweet thoughts, tingled with the memories of the day, those sad romantic sentiments aroused by the vivid history of bygone happenings of long ago. Perhaps I should not have gone. I suppose I shall pay for it with extra heartache, but somehow I did not think it would be like this.

During the remainder of the drive back only Charmian and Henri chattered. Julia was kept silent by a sense of defeat. Paul was quiet through anger. How dare Julia take it upon herself to discuss his supposed thoughts on love with Charmian.

Gaston met them at the door of the apartment, saying that M'm'selle Georgette had called for her brother and sister and was waiting in the salon. While he was speaking Georgette, wearing a lovely fur coat, came to the door of the salon. She greeted Paul warmly, holding out both white hands to him in welcome, then asked the children if they were ready to leave. She took no notice of Julia who hesitated in the background uncertain whether to retire to her room, or to follow the others into the salon for the apéritif Paul had promised them all as they came up in the lift.

Paul had dropped Georgette's hands, then observing that she took no notice of Julia, he said pointedly, " I think you two have met before."

Georgette looked vague. " Have we? . . . Oh, yes, I remember now. *Bon soir,* Mademoiselle Brown." Her eyes were cold and her manner distant. Julia felt the chilly atmosphere. She bowed in acknowledgement, and Georgette said, " I hope the children have not bothered you too much today?"

" They were no bother at all, Mademoiselle Georgette."

The children looked owlishly from one grown up's face to the other, while Georgette talked to Paul, excluding Julia, who turned quietly to leave the room.

It was Henri who stopped her. He put his arm around Julia's waist.

" Oh no you don't, Julia. She must stay here, Uncle Paul, must she not?"

Paul paused. He saw Henri's arm around Julia's waist. The familiar attitude annoyed him. He spoke sharply, " She will do what she pleases, Henri."

Julia put up her hand and loosened Henri's clasp. " Then I think I will go to my room for I am very tired," she said softly.

She bowed to Georgette who was watching her with stormy eyes, then shook hands with Charmian, the baby. "*Au revoir.* I hope we may meet again before you return to Canada."

" Do you mean that, Julia?" asked Charmian.

" Sure, she does," Henri replied.

Chapter Ten

PAUL TOOK Georgette, her sister and brother home. Julia did not see him again that evening. She concluded that Paul had been pressed to stay to dinner.

Indeed, Julia did not see him for several days, and then he treated her with such cold formality that she longed to ask him what she had done to offend him. But past experience had taught her that she usually got the worst on those occasions, so she pretended not to notice Paul's coldness and reserve. When they met, their relations were strictly on business terms, impersonal and polite.

At Christmas Paul warmed to her a little. He gave her a large phial of some heavenly perfume Julia had often wished for but could not afford to buy.

" I could have written a nice message on the label, but I had no idea what to say. At this season when presents are packed so prettily it would be natural to write, ' To Julia with love.' It would have been a charming sentiment. I did not dare to do so for I was afraid you might remind me that love is not to be bought or had for the asking, or begged for. It just happens. I suppose people think it strange that it has not happened to us. We are too sensible. Neither of us would dream of permitting himself to be involved. I am your boss and you are my too useful secretary. We are a businesslike pair. Not that any soft feeling between us would mean the sack for you. On the contrary, I should welcome such a show. It would show me that you are human."

Julia listened in silence. The present in its pink paper covering tied with a French blue ribbon was on her desk between them. She could read his handwriting on the label. " Mademoiselle Brown." Her hand rested idly on the desk.

Suddenly Paul raised his hand and covered hers, squeezing it a little.

" You do understand what I am getting at, do you not? I was too angry to speak about it before, but I am calmer now."

Julia pulled her hand away. " I do understand, perfectly, monsieur." She had flushed deeply though, whether because of what he said, or that he touched her hand Paul did not know. Obviously it was mortifying to know that he had heard and remembered all Charmian's silly talk.

She said in a low voice, " There was no need for you to be angry with anyone."

" There seemed to be at the time. I have often wondered : did you really mean what you said to Charmian, or were you trying to kill that silly crush she imagines she has for me? It is Christmas and a time for forgiveness. You know I will forgive you anything. It hurts when you treat me coldly."

Julia did not answer because she could think of nothing useful to say.

" Look at me, Mademoiselle Brown."

Slowly Julia raised her eyes to his. What she saw in his made her smile. Paul grinned in reply.

" What do you think?" she breathed, and her heart thudded madly in her breast.

" At this precise moment I think you are a witch. But whatever there is or is not between us, we are not so sensible after all."

" It is Christmas, and I love Christmas wishes," she said, and there was a hint of coquetry in her manner.

He took out his fountain pen. " Then I shall write, ' To Julia with love.' "

He picked up the parcel and turned over the label.

" Please."

They spent the whole of Christmas Day in Paul's apartment. Julia had a few greetings cards from London and a couple of presents, but Paul was popular, and though his country did not " keep " Christmas as English people do he had many parcels from all over the world. He insisted on Julia opening some of them. " You shall have as your share all those not suitable for men," he promised.

The mood lasted well into the new year. To Julia these days seemed full of portent, and each morning a sense of fear and disaster increased.

Then one evening what she had been waiting for happened.

Paul came in early. He spoke to her abruptly, his manner as distant and repellent as it had ever been. He said, " The merger has gone through to your uncle's great satisfaction. Your uncle and cousin remain on the Board. Your uncle is vice-president of the group of companies that are now linked together. Your cousin is general-manager, though *he* is on trial. Does that suit you?"

Julia's eyes shone with joy. So great was her relief that all would now be well for her uncle that she scarcely noticed

that the man who had arranged all this was in a towering
rage. "Oh, I am so glad. I am sure my people are overjoyed."

"Are you? The whole thing has been arranged with you
in mind. Don't forget that."

"I am only a small shareholder."

"Maybe. You can look upon it as your gift to them."

"Gift! Surely that is the wrong word? Isn't it a business
deal between you and them?"

"You can put it that way if you like."

Julia paused and stared wide-eyed at Paul's face. There
was something inimical in his tone. She did not like the way
he spoke. It was as though he were hurling stones at her.
She said, "Please, would you speak more plainly, monsieur?"

"It is quite simple. This is something you have
wanted over many months, and now you have won your
way."

"But you must have thought it a good thing, too. You
are a business man and would hardly entertain a proposition
you knew to be unsound."

"I am not sure that it is a good thing for anyone. Certainly without your direct intervention I should have re-
jected the idea in the beginning." Paul's tone was harder
now. There was a rasp in it that warned her she must be
tactful. "It is not even businesslike."

"Oh, then it is something you have done personally for
my sake, and *I* have to thank *you*?"

"Entirely. Thanking me will show your appreciation."

Julia hesitated. When she spoke her voice quivered with
emotion. "Of course I thank you and so will my uncle.
You have relieved us of a terrible load of worry. I know
nothing about the appreciation-value and will leave that to
my uncle and cousin. But when you meet, and you must do
so soon, I warn you that my uncle is an upright man. Whatever the circumstances, I do not believe my uncle would
want your charity."

"It is not a word I like using, but charity is a good word for this."

Julia's chin shot up. She felt rigid with sudden anger. She asked swiftly, "Then why did you do it for them?"

Paul gestured wearily. "I have told you. To please you. You wanted it."

"Frankly I don't know much about it. I brought the matter to your notice because I was told it was a good thing and you would be glad I put you on to it."

Paul laughed angrily. "Who told you? No, do not answer, I know. You were out to please that cousin of yours. You had a swollen idea of his capabilities. It gave you a kick to see him through rose-coloured glasses."

"Don't be ridiculous. Andrew *is* clever," Julia cried hotly.

"Maybe, but he's a fool in business. Of course you think he is wonderful because you are blindly, madly in love with him."

Paul paused wishing he could recall those wild words. He had not meant to say as much. He blamed an inward consuming jealousy for driving him to say things which might be wiser left unsaid. Anyway it was out now, and he was glad. If he had had to bottle it up much longer he would have gone mad.

Julia flashed, "Of course I love Andrew."

"*Dieu*! You have the impertinence to tell me you are in love. How dare you!"

"You said I was first."

Paul was beside himself with rage. "So now we have the truth at last. This Andrew whom you love has a good position as manager of three companies, all of which will be ruined by him in no time at all. Now you can marry him. He will not mind that you have lived in my apartment solely for the purpose of leading me step by step to buy up a few rotten companies, sink some money into them, and put *him* on his feet. All this of course if I can perform a miracle."

"That was not true. Andrew did mind my coming here.

He was set against the idea. There is no need for you to be insulting either."

Paul laughed—an unhappy sound.

Julia went close to him. She stood straight as a ramrod in front of him. She had no fear of him at this moment. Her eyes were glowing with anger. Never had she disliked a man so much. Words burst from her in a torrent.

She cried, " I have something to remind you, too. All this company business cropped up *after* you brought me here, not because you really needed a woman secretary. A man would have fitted into this household better than a woman. You would not have had to go out so much for meals. But you did not mind that. You were burnt up with the idea of humiliating *one* girl because another girl had turned you down. Any girl would have suited your purpose. It was just bad luck for me that I turned up. You took your revenge out on me. That was a nice thing to do, wasn't it? It has shown me how rotten you are. You know as well as I do what people think of us, yet not once have you told me to go, which you should have done. You talk glibly of my marrying Andrew. You don't know what you are saying. Andrew was married yesterday to a girl I have never met. If you care to look in the English papers this morning you will see an announcement of his marriage."

Her limbs were trembling and she sank down on the nearest chair. She could not look at Paul for she still burned with white-hot rage against him. She took a deep steadying breath—several of them. Well, now she had said her say and this must be the end. She waited for him to speak. Within seconds now she would probably be packing to go. It was a steadying thought.

Paul was going to shout back at Julia. He was about to tell her to clear out of his apartment at once, that he was tired of her and never wished to see her again. She was only a nuisance value to him, when it dawned upon him that Julia had said Andrew was married.

He paused nonplussed, and as the full meaning of the

words registered, he stammered, "You do not seem to care?" His voice was changed. It was as though a fever had left him, and his eyes which a moment before had looked so wild, were calm again.

"Of course I don't. I have never loved Andrew in that way. It is only you who thought I did." She spoke impatiently, feeling that Paul should never have asked her such a stupid question.

She was astonished when Paul hid his face in his hands for a moment. "*Bon dieu!*" he cried. "What misery have I made for myself?"

"You must take the blame for humiliating me, too, monsieur," she told him grimly. "I do not forget having seen the sly looks your friends have given me when they visited you here. I observed how Mademoiselle Georgette drew aside her skirt from me that day we returned from Versailles and found her here calling for her brother and sister. She would have ignored me entirely only you forced her hand. Even then her voice and cold manner measured the distance between us. That hurt very much. She thought I was your mistress."

Paul was silent. He had realised all that at the time, and hoped that Julia had not, but he was mistaken. He had tried never to let that sort of thing happen again, for *he did not wish this girl to leave him now.*

After a while he said, "You see so much, then you must have noticed lately that I do not invite my friends to this apartment any more. It is so that you shall not be exposed to that sort of thing."

Julia brushed that aside. "Oh, I don't expect you to cut yourself off from your friends on my account. This is your home and your life. I must not interfere. Surely it would be better for me to find a small apartment for myself near here? I could come in daily. That is, unless you wish me to return to London?"

Paul put up his hand imperiously. "I shall not allow that. You stay here."

Julia's pretty lips twisted. "And continue to be humiliated? Oh, no monsieur! That will not do for me." She spoke proudly, and oddly, it was Paul who felt humiliated.

Hitherto Paul had been so angry he had spoken in French, but now that he was calmer he said earnestly in English, "Do not talk like that any more. I promise that you shall never have cause to complain of such humiliation again. It is not a nice word, anyway. Indeed as we are the only ones who know the truth we realise what nonsense it is."

"You have asked my pardon before, monsieur."

Paul frowned, trying to recall instances of what Julia meant. Her accusation perplexed him and he said, reasonably enough, "I do not think I have failed you. I try to foresee adverse circumstances, and show thoughtfulness for your comfort, though I am unable always to govern them, but I am not unmindful of the distress some people have caused you. Try to remember that the French look upon some things differently from the English."

He spoke so seriously and seemed so contrite that Julia, who now longed to forgive him everything when they could perhaps start afresh with a new friendship, found herself relenting. Also she was sensitive to the change in Paul since she told him about Andrew's marriage. She longed to be sweet and soft to him, to show in little things that she liked him. Paul might take advantage of her weakness, for that was what it amounted to. Yet because she loved him so dearly, and longed to stay with him in his apartment, even under the humiliating conditions that occasionally upset her, as they had lately; and because more than anything she hoped some day he would love her as much as she adored him and life without him would not be worthwhile, she relented visibly.

She smiled up at him, then lowered her eyes quickly in case he should read the melting tenderness in hers.

He took both her hands in his and squeezed them hard.

" But this is the last time, monsieur," she said frankly in a low tone which trembled in spite of her efforts to steady it. " There is a limit to what I can take."

Brave words, because in her heart Julia knew that if Paul caused her the same pain again and asked forgiveness she would give it again and yet again. Julia acknowledged to herself, " I have been too soft already."

Paul let go her hands. " Of course. I promise to be extra good from now on. Are we friends again?"

" I suppose so."

" That is said grudgingly."

" Because I am not sure of you, monsieur."

" I see." He began to pace restlessly to and fro in the room. " Then I must try to prove myself." He sighed heavily several times, but he did not say why, and presently he left the room.

Long afterwards, when thinking over this frank and stormy talk in the quiet of the night, Paul recalled Julia's words ". . . . Not once have you told me to go, which you should have done! " That was true, but Julia knew the position as well as he did. She must have realised how her good name had suffered. Perhaps she had relied on the true position between them, which only they knew, and trusted to his decency in taking good care of her. Anyhow she had not packed up and left the apartment. She was free to go. He could not have stopped her. That made her equally to blame.

Thoughts such as these milled around in his head until his brain felt on fire and further sleep was impossible. He got out of bed and pulled on his dressing-gown. Drawing back the curtains that seemed to shroud his windows day and night, which shut out the sounds of traffic passing ceaselessly below, but also shut out light and air, he opened the windows wide and watched the dawn lightening the sky in the east, and spread until he could distinguish well-known landmarks rising like mirages out of the early ground mists.

While a sense of peace stole over him he tried to fathom what was in his mind and heart. His nerves which had been dithery after the stormy talk with Julia, gained some measure of peace, steadied by something in his mind, the reasoning that comes with silence and being alone. He had a longing during that lonely vigil to take care of Julia, a desire to take her in his arms and comfort her. It was a fiercer need than he had ever felt for Chantal, who compared with Julia as a diamond, hard, brilliant, scintillating, to a soft lustrous pearl.

He thought of what it lay in Julia's power to do. She might leave him. The fact that some day soon matters might shape themselves in such a way that change of some sort would be imperative, caused him fresh anguish. She must never go. He wanted her to stay.

The old fear that if left to herself, if she had an apartment out, Julia might find someone else to love her and leave him as abruptly as Chantal had gone, made him tremble.

Chantal had filled his heart and mind once. Only a year ago he had been besottedly in love with her. When Chantal left him for another he vowed no other girl should enter his heart.

Normal life such as any man might expect, to marry and have children, was over for him. He had no intention of ever marrying. The future had stretched before him like a great black void. In his bitter anger he decided that no other girl should be given the chance of treating him as Chantal had. To prove his strength to himself he had taken an attractive girl into his apartment and secretly dared either of them, Chantal or Julia, ever to cause him to change his mind.

For a while he had been satisfied.

Lately Paul realised that he had only been recovering from the shock of the blow. He was anything but satisfied. Having a lovely girl living at the end of a passage in his home only caused him discontent. He wanted something more. It made him irritable that he could not have that something.

Julia had never even attempted to storm his heart. She had never tried to tempt him. She was naturally feminine though it had never seemingly occurred to her to use any of her feminine wiles on him.

Yet Julia was in his heart. He recognised that this dawn.

How it had happened he did not know, except that the change had come gradually. She had neither stormed his heart or tempted him. It had been more subtle than that. Julia had crept in, so quietly and softly, so mouselike, that he had not noticed what was happening to him until it was too late.

He had fought against the knowledge. He hated the idea of two women in his life. He had been rude and quarrelsome to Julia as he had never thought to be to any woman. He had even hoped to drive her away. He had known of her loneliness, yet had done nothing to help her. She must have been unhappy. He realised that, and had exulted because someone was suffering as he had. Then he had tried running off to South America and to Canada, pleading business as the excuse to get away from that deadly cloying hold on his heart. He had, as she said, humiliated her. He had hated rivals, his friends—Andrew Lester. He had ruthlessly broken across that friendship, for what it was worth. But whatever he said or did, whether he went away or remained in Paris, whether indeed if they met or not during the day, he could not forget Julia or get her image out of his mind. Paul had never known himself like this. He was dissatisfied, jumpy and quarrelsome, and nothing would ever make him feel differently.

And now this impasse. He had a feeling of doom from which there was no escape.

Fires were being lighted. The atmosphere smelled smoky. It was cold and he shivered. The experts had prophesied snow. Suddenly he closed the windows and drew the curtains. He felt the radiators. They were lukewarm. But he felt better for the fresh air and returning to bed he slept until Gaston called him later in the morning. But Paul was still undecided, still wondering about the scheme of fate in relation to himself. He was tired of being hurt.

Chapter Eleven

FOR A month a strange peace hung over the apartment. It was like a truce in a great battle, when each side pauses to take stock of what he has won, what he wants in the near future, and what ammunition he has left to get it.

Paul was an exemplary employer overnight. He was a strictly impersonal and businesslike employer. He was especially impersonal in office hours. Breaking the habit of his lifetime in business he seldom asked Julia to " take a note " outside office hours. Though she had not minded some overtime. Paul was scrupulous about sticking to working hours. He considered Julia's comfort. If she had a feminine wish to deck out the salon like a boudoir instead of an office he suggested she should buy some flowers at the florist's around the corner and charge them to his account. The only proviso Paul made was not to overdo the decoration because the perfume in the centrally-heated atmosphere made him feel sick. If Julia wished to go out in the evening he made it easy for her to cease work early, himself arranging with Gaston for a tray of food and hot coffee to be waiting for her return. He gave her tickets for the theatre, yet never once suggested accompanying her. When Julia developed a cold he sent for the doctor. When she protested saying she had only a head cold, he retorted, " It might be the beginning of something serious. Neglected colds lead to pneumonia."

The only thing Paul withheld from her was his own companionship.

All this V.I.P. treatment was pleasant and acceptable for a short while, but there came a time when Julia wearied of this strange truce. She, too, felt unsatisfied, cheated at times, even hungry, and inclined to blame Paul because there was no need to remain so aloof. He was going too far.

Julia knew what all this absurd isolation meant. Paul was trying to prove to her that because she lived under his roof that did not mean she must be his mistress. She had known all that before, but she could not come out into the open and tell his friends that, surely the whole point of this exact employer and employee business. So soon the whole idea savoured of the ridiculous. Far from wanting to laugh, though she could see the funny youthful side of it, Julia longed to call everything off that Paul had arranged and say, " Let's be as we were at the beginning. I miss our squabbles. At least they were healthy and understandable. Let's have a grand row, for then I understand you and I know where I am."

Unfortunately the new Paul was unapproachable. Even in his mildest moods she could learn nothing fresh of him. It was exasperating.

Julia observed, too, that Gaston and Marie were puzzled and uneasy, for they appeared quieter than usual these days.

There was an occasion when Paul showed up as a human being instead of an automaton. It was a cold day in February. Julia, recovered from her cold, had gone out for her daily morning walk. It began to snow heavily while she was out, and she arrived home covered in a white mantle.

She stamped off most of the snow on the mat outside the door, but her cap and face were wet with melting snow. She paused to beat her cold hands together.

As she was doing this, she heard the door open, and looking up saw Paul standing in the doorway. She smiled involuntarily and surprised an answering smile in his eyes. He opened wide the door, and as she passed in, glad of the warmth of the apartment that at once encompassed her shivering form he said, " I heard you beating time on the mat. You must be frozen. Snow is coming down heavily."

He closed the door and helped her off with her coat. Then struck by its light weight he exclaimed quickly in some concern, " Have you no warmer coat than this which is no earthly use in snow? It is as thin as paper and no protection against bitter winter cold."

" I have a heavier one but it is such a weight I seldom wear it," she told him.

" If you are determined to go out in the cold early morning you must. You will catch your death of cold this weather." Then he said, " I will give this to Gaston to dry off for you. Perhaps Marie has some bouillon prepared."

" Oh, please, don't fuss. I've often been far wetter than this and no one has minded."

" Then it is high time someone did. Go into the salon and unfreeze."

So while Julia, wondering, but pleased to be taken care of, went into the salon, Paul carried her coat and cap to the kitchen.

Presently he came back and read Julia a lecture about the need of keeping warm in winter. Gaston brought in a tray with two cups of brown bouillon on it.

" Marie wondered, m'sieu'—" His hesitancy created a tension.

Paul laughed. " I am not surprised. I never drink anything during the morning, but I will certainly drink this. It smells good."

Paul and Julia drank the bouillon, and somehow the slight tension disappeared.

"Now shall we begin work?" Paul suggested, when he saw a pink colour steal into her cheeks. "Sure you are warm enough to type correctly?"

"Oh, yes, thank you, monsieur. Feel," and she stretched out her hands towards him. "I am quite hot."

Paul made no attempt to touch her, only looked woodenly at the white hands with the pretty pink-tipped fingernail, just under his eyes. "I shall take your word for that," he said.

He picked up some mail. "Despite the snowstorms which I hear are widespread, cutting out any flying today, this bunch managed to get through."

The snow had deadened all sound of traffic. The central heating was turned full on. Paul was ready for work.

Only Julia behaved oddly. She was warmed and now felt sleepy. Her thoughts were hazy.

"Would you like to rest Mademoiselle Brown?"

"No, thank you. I am quite all right."

"Sure?"

"Quite sure."

"Then suppose you make the effort to wake up, and let us get down to work."

The asperity in his voice woke Julia up.

February came to an end, and March came in with winds of gale force—soon it would be April—and then May—

Idly Julia raised the loose leaves of a calendar on her desk. May! Could she stand a spring in Paris, near Paul, and not give herself away?

With a kind of anguish of despair she thought fiercely, How can *you* stand it, Paul? Are you so inhuman that you are insensitive to my plight? I have worked so hard to make you love me. What can I now do to turn your heart towards me? I can't go on like this much longer. I cannot endure this waiting—getting nowhere. Her mind was in a state of eternal confusion. It was seething with unrest and the weariness of unrequited love when, one morning, Paul did not come into the salon to read the mail she had piled neatly on the open wire tray for him to read.

Julia did some other work, then listened. The apartment was as quiet as usual. Suddenly, a little disquieted, she went into the kitchen and asked Gaston if Monsieur had already gone out.

Gaston's expression was sad. As he usually smiled at her this was a bad omen.

"M'sieu' is in bed, M'm'selle. He has *la grippe*."

"Oh, is he very bad?" she asked quickly, her worst fears aroused.

"It is no good, but the doctor, who has already been, says that he will be better soon."

"Can I do anything for him?"

"It is all taken care of, M'm'selle."

Four days later, an eternity to Julia, Gaston reported that M'sieu' was well again. After *déjeuner* he asked Julia to listen for M'sieu's bell while he went out to do some shopping. "Marie, too, has a little migraine. She is in bed, but she will be okay by this evening."

"You are leaving me in charge?"

"If you will have the kindness, M'm'selle."

The apartment was quiet and peaceful. Twice the doorbell rang and Julia answered it. She looked in to see Marie, gave her a fresh hot water bottle and a glass of Schweppes and returned to the salon.

Then what she had both dreaded and longed to hear happened.

Monsieur's bell rang.

With some trepidation and a fluttering heart Julia knocked on Paul's bedroom door.

"*Entrez!*" There was the old familiar impatient rasp in his voice.

The room was in a twilight of gloom, but in the half-light she could make out Paul's tall figure lying on his back in the bed. One arm was raised, the back of his hand covering his eyes. As Julia entered, hearing the sound, Paul lifted his hand and saw her.

He had been sleeping, but he was wide awake now.

"Oh, it's you," he exclaimed. "What are you doing here?"

"You rang the bell, monsieur."

"Where is Gaston?"

"He had to do some shopping."

"What is Marie doing?"

"She has one of her migraines."

"Oh well, you have no right to be in here. The next thing is that you will go down with *la grippe*."

"I hope not; but someone has to look after you. How are you?"

"Much better, thank you. I am to get up tomorrow. The next day I roam the apartment. The following day I go out, and Monday we begin work again."

Julia eyed him doubtfully. "I do not think your convalescence will be as quick as that."

"Then you do not know me."

She smiled. "You are certainly full of surprises."

He smiled back. "It is good of you to take so much trouble over me," he told her.

Julia came over to the bed and stood looking down at him. His face was grey and drawn. He had evidently been through it, and she thought he was thinner.

"What about a drink?" she said. "Gaston has made some more for you."

"It depends what sort of drink."

"A soft fruit—iced."

"Oh, that! I have drunk litres of that stuff the last four days."

"It does you good."

"Nonsense, it is poison to me."

" Don't you want to get well?"

" Certainly . . . All right, give me some. It shows how good I am to take it."

Julia went over to the table and poured out some fruit drink and handed it to him. At that moment she forgot herself, wanting only to see Paul himself again, and ready to give him comfort and help.

He took the glass, but could not drink it easily, so she slipped an arm under his pillow and held his head up a little while she raised the glass to his lips.

He was slow drinking, but when he had had enough she asked him to hold his position while she plumped up his pillows afresh. When this was done she lowered his head on to the pillow, and he sank back thankfully.

" Is that more comfortable?"

" Much better. You are a born nurse. You seem to know what I want by instinct."

" Now rest and go to sleep again."

" But I have been sleeping on and off all day. The room is rather dark. I suppose you will not pull back the curtains? Daylight is so much more cheerful than this twilight. It is Gaston's idea to shroud the windows, not mine."

" I hate being shut in myself. I never like my curtains pulled over." She opened the curtains. " Is that better?"

" Much. There is quite a good view from my window. It seems so silly to shut it out. You have a poor view from your window, I recall."

" Mostly chimney pots and roofs. There is a wedge of sky, too. Sometimes I see stars."

" No sun?"

" Very little."

" Poor you! "

" Marie says I am lucky because even my small room is expensive in Paris."

" Maybe." He seemed to ponder over this.

" Anyway I like my room."

Julia tidied the sheet and drew the blanket up under his chin. Then she said, " Now I must go."

" Do not go yet! "

" I must or you'll never settle to sleep. Marie and Gaston will scold me."

" Do you mind?"

" Yes, if it interferes with your getting better."

Paul laughed saying, " I do believe you wish me to be well."

" You know I do. *Au revoir,* monsieur. I shall not be disturbing you again this afternoon."

" You have never disturbed me. I am all the better for your visit."

She turned to leave him, but even as she did so, Paul's hand moved, and he took her fingers and held them for a short while against his cheek. She saw that his eyes were closed. " You are a wonderful person," he said. " I feel quite well again, since I have had this little chat with you."

She had flushed at the little caress. Now she drew her hand away from his, aware that his touch had confused her. She switched on a small bedside lamp and left him.

Outside the door Julia paused and put her hand over her heart. Paul wasn't, she thought, like any other man she had ever met. That was why she supposed she had always had a special feeling for him whatever his moods. She loved Paul for something in himself that appealed to her. It did not matter how he expressed himself, whether he was angry or in a good temper. He was Paul. Mostly he had been self-sufficient. That was when he was well. Today she had seen him in a new guise. He was still ill and pathetically dependent on Gaston and Marie who, though they were devoted, had an interest in keeping him alive, for they obtained their livelihood from him. It was different with her. Such service as she was able to render was because she enjoyed comforting, cosseting the weak. It made her happy to help him not because he was her boss, but because she loved him dearly.

Later she went back to his room, not knocking, but listening outside to the unbroken quiet within, then opening the door to see if all was well.

She heard his voice saying, " Is that you, Mademoiselle?" He did not move, or appear to look at her.

" Yes, monsieur. Are you all right?"

" Quite."

" I am glad."

" Is Gaston back?"

" No, monsieur, but Marie is better."

" *Bon.* Then go to bed yourself and try to get a good night's rest."

" I do not need much sleep."

" I am sure you do, otherwise you will lose the freshness from your beauty."

She felt oddly pleased at the compliment. Then she said, " *Bon soir, monsieur*—"

" *Bon soir, Mademoiselle.*" His voice was drowsy and she had the feeling that he had kept awake thinking she might come in again.

Chapter Twelve

AFTER A cold hard winter Spring came in with a rush. One morning, when the lime trees in the Champs Elysées had uncurled their light green leaves, the river had lost its steely sheen and mirrored the clear blue sky, and Julia was feeling bored with the pattern of her life, things changed. They did not change as she might have expected. Gaston brought a note from Paul. It was on the tray with her *petit-déjeuner*. It was from Paul, and read tersely, " Please see me before I leave for the City office at nine o'clock. P.R." Julia had had such notes before, usually reminders to see Paul about some problem before he left for his office.

Gaston waited for a reply, and Julia said, " Tell Monsieur that I will be in the salon at a quarter to nine."

" *Oui, m'm'selle,*" replied Gaston and left the room.

Punctually Julia opened the door of the salon. At the same moment Paul came out of his bedroom. He had long ago recovered completely from his illness. He looked debonair as usual in a new check tweed suit, and seeing this Julia thought with dismay, He's going into the country! Her spirits fell because now she would not catch even a glimpse of him all day, but she smiled a little as her eyes met his, saying, " *Bonjour, monsieur.*"

" *Bonjour, Mademoiselle Brown.*" He put some letters on her desk, and gave a few directions how she should answer them. But his manner was preoccupied and she guessed that the letters were not the reason he wanted to see her before leaving for the City. She observed, too, by the way he walked over to the window, and looked out, his hands in his trouser pockets jingling some loose keys and coins. Then for no reason at all Julia suddenly panicked, wondering if he were going to give her the sack. She recalled that lately her work had been eased, she had many free hours, especially in the afternoons, when she could do as she pleased.

With hands pressed tightly together in her lap she waited for Paul to speak. At first he did not seem to notice her patience, but at length he said quickly over his shoulder,

" I thought of giving a small dinner party here tomorrow evening—just you, myself and a couple of friends, a husband and wife. I am wondering if you will be kind enough to be hostess for me."

Julia was so relieved that her dark fears meant nothing, she said generously, " Why yes, monsieur."

" It is rather an important dinner. These two old friends are passing through Paris, and such an opportunity of seeing them may never occur again. It will be rather formal. I shall wear a black tie, but I hope you will wear your best dress. Will you arrange some flowers for the table with the colour of your dress in mind? I especially wish you to make a good impression."

He seemed labouring under some strain, finding difficulty with his English, and relapsing into French.

Julia nodded. Her brown eyes were enormous in the morning light. She was wondering what was behind all this, sure that presently she would know.

She said, " I will do my best."

" You have good taste so I know that I can safely leave the flowers to you. My guests will arrive soon after eight for dinner at eight-thirty. I have already consulted Marie and Gaston about the menu, the food and wine and the silver I want used."

" It sounds exciting," Julia told him happily, glad that there was to be a break in the monotony of her evenings, and delighted that Paul would be with them. It was a long while since he had given even a little dinner party in the salon.

Paul turned round and looked at her with penetrating eyes.

" I do not know about excitement for you. It is import-ant to me, and I hope you will have a pleasant evening."

" I am sure of it."

She seemed so positive, and he paused wondering how to phrase his surprise for her, certain that she might not like the proposition after all.

Then he said unexpectedly, " You have not yet asked me the names of my guests."

" Do I know them?" It occurred to her that probably she did not. She smiled wisely at him. The times he had brought friends to dine in the apartment! They were charming people, but Julia met them for dinner and never saw them again.

Paul came over to her and said deliberately, " It is my former secretary, Chantal and her husband."

There was a tense feeling in the atmosphere. Julia's smile faded.

" Oh!" she breathed. " I never thought I should meet them."

" I did not think it possible either. But señor rang me

up yesterday and said they were in Paris for a few days before going on to Rome and I decided to ask them to dinner. You do not seem very pleased, mademoiselle?"

"No," cried Julia. "I—don't pretend to be. I wonder, would it be possible for you to arrange for another hostess? I mean I would see that the table is laid exactly as you wish. I would buy and arrange the flowers, but I do not wish to meet Madame."

"That is absurd," said Paul quickly. "You have never seen Chantal so how can you possibly object to meeting her? Even you would admit she is beautiful."

"I have heard of her, and I do not want to meet her," Julia said stubbornly. She could not look at Paul and hide her emotion from him.

"But why? Give me one sensible reason and I will not bother you further."

"Because—" she was beginning reluctantly when she paused. It would not be easy to tell Monsieur that she was insanely jealous of Chantal's beauty, or her hold over him, and she could not meet his former friend, she had not the courage.

She thought in quick anguish, It isn't fair. He should not ask me to meet her. I can't do it. This really is beyond me.

Aloud she said rather sulkily, "I have no desire ever to meet Madame."

As she spoke Julia was conscious of a certain quick anger against Paul for exposing her to the humiliation of meeting his former love.

She was frightened, too, because Paul had forgotten his promise not to humiliate her further so quickly. He had remembered Chantal, too, and Julia felt how hopeless it was trying to fight for a love that he had long ago given to another. But he might have spared her some thought.

How can he be so insensitive? Even if he can never love me surely he must know what any girl would feel at meeting someone so much lovelier than herself? Why should I be expected to enjoy a pleasant evening playing second fiddle to her beauty? What right has he to expect me to be his hostess, as though I am a dummy with no feelings at all? She's got everything, beautiful clothes, fabulous jewels, perfumes, to enhance her loveliness, while I have only one secondhand model and no jewels. How could I hope to compete with her?

Julia did not think this is self-pity, but with a certain anger.

She was uneasy, too, for the hope which she had tried to keep alive in her heart that some day she would win Paul's love, seemed faint. What was wrong with her that Paul was so unresponsive?

Something of this smouldering rebellion against Paul and fate must have shown on Julia's face, for Paul said, " I beg of you as a special favour to me, to change your mind, Miss Brown."

" You promised never to expose me to this kind of thing again. I relied on your word," Julia flashed.

" I do not think I am exposing you to anything horrid. I have not forgotten what I said. I shall be there anyway. You are in no danger." He spoke quietly, even coldly, then went on, " However, if you are really set against pleasing me, please forget that I have spoken. But I shall never ask a favour of you again."

A shiver of fear shook her, and with the fear came regret that he was so unresponsive. She was afraid suddenly because his words made her realise that her stay in Paris was shortening. She had always known that an end might come which would leave her unhappy, but she had refused to dwell on that dreary aspect. Perhaps this was the end, the pointers said so, only something within her would not let her recognise it? With that knowledge in her mind, Julia felt brave enough to say to him, " It isn't a question of pleasing you this time, monsieur. I am thinking of myself when I say that everything within me rebels against meeting Madame."

" I would like to understand your reasoning, Miss Brown, but I cannot," Paul said sadly, and it was as though he, too,

F

knew that the end of the old relationship between them was not far off.

Julia was silent because there was nothing useful she could think of to say.

She was thinking, He is terribly disappointed at not getting his own way. Now everything is lost for me. He will never forgive me. A kind of anguish swept over her making her feel faint. He doesn't understand. He never will now. I suppose any other girl would have called up all the fortitude she possessed to please him, but I can't. I'm too weak to act a part successfully. Besides, I'm too tired. It was bad enough fighting a losing game for him, but to fight against her hold on him is madness. I just could not do it.

A little frightened now at having burnt all her boats too completely with a flat refusal which Julia could see by his face angered him, Julia said faintly, " I knew it would be impossible for you to understand, but honestly I would rather not meet her."

For a moment, Paul looked stern and unapproachable. He paused, raising his shirt cuff with slender fingers as he looked at his wristwatch and said, " Maybe you are right. Maybe *I* am. I should have spoken to you last night, when we both had more time to discuss your problem. I am late now. Think over what I have said during the day, Miss Brown, and we will continue our talk tonight. I will dine here with you if that will help." He turned away saying in a matter of fact voice which sounded more like a phlegmatic Englishman than a volatile Frenchman, " I could ask someone else to play hostess for me, Georgette, for instance, but unfortunately neither she nor anyone else can take your place. Any other night perhaps, but not this special night."

Julia did not speak. She could only look at him. She felt weary of fighting him, sick at heart because she could not manage her own affairs, something other people did easily —like Chantal, who had taken advantage of all that Paul could give while waiting for her own Prince Charming to appear. If there had been complications, Chantal had made short work of them.

Paul seemed a closed book to Julia. If he had a plan in life, he had never revealed it to her. She had had to be content with fourth-hand scraps of gossip. She admitted she did not know the real Paul at all. She had lived under his roof, yet they had enjoyed few of those small intimate things which are supposed to make for friendship. She had little knowledge of the hidden fund of kindness, strength and consideration which she sometimes suspected lay under the surface. There had been memories, good and bad, yet few kind remembrances, so little to build on.

Until lately there had been hope in Julia's heart that all would miraculously change. It was changing only not for the best, certainly not conforming to her wishes. If anything Paul, instead of expanding their friendship, retreated more and yet more into his shell, until even what Julia learnt about him took on the aspect of a dream.

He actually appeared content with his lot. There were fewer signs of short temper or resentment against Fate. That he could be tender, Julia well knew. What Julia did not know was that somewhere deep inside Paul, the old fires of vitality, love and passion were stirring to active life again; and that his reason for seeking her company more often than before was a genuine desire to be with her.

So blinded was Julia by her own apparent failure she did not realise what was happening under her nose.

During the day her mind dithered. At times she decided to end all the fuss and go away. I can't stand it any longer, she thought once, then later, struggling to believe in herself she thought rebelliously, Why should this end? Why must I go away? Why should I give him up? He is sure to turn to me if I impose my will on him, not obviously of course, but tactfully. Yet even as she thought thus Julia knew in the bottom of her heart that she had nothing on which to base her hopes, that the parting was coming closer, that the end of this curious friendship was only a matter of time, and that terrible fear of facing up to the end overwhelmed her once more. She cried, but that of course did no good and only made her eyes red, when she had a desire to lock herself in her room and see no one. But that would be silly for Paul, when he came in, might come along to her room himself, insist on seeing her, even capable of breaking down the door if she refused.

By evening Julia was lonely, depressed and undecided what to do. She had finished crying and her nerves were numb.

Paul came in the evening, too. He brought her a bunch of flowers wrapped in cellophane as a kind of peace offering. As he put them in her lap with a smile she had the feeling of being trapped.

She recoiled but she guessed that he was standing close to her studying her face as though he would read the decision of her thoughts in her expression, and purposely she made her expression blank.

She thought rebelliously, He's not going to buy my consent with flowers. I'm not giving in to him so easily. Why should I? He can't really expect it.

Or did he? With a beautiful sense of proportion coupled with his shrewd business acumen, Paul was allowing the flowers to plead his cause.

He said suddenly, " You have been crying."

" What a silly thing to say! "

" It is a silly thing to do. There is no need for you to cry. We will have dinner first, before we settle down to talk. Is that right?"

She sighed. " Yes," and she wished the matter could be shelved for ever.

At dinner which was eaten by candlelight, Julia found herself watching him closely, examining his features, hoping to retain a memory of something she might never see again after tonight. Now that the evening was here, and nothing settled which she was supposed to have been busy settling during the day, a queer fatalistic mood came over her. This

is the end, she thought. It is here. For Paul was not the kind
of man to allow a mass of unravelled problems to clutter up
his life. He would never let things drift. Having told her to
think things out, he would conclude she had done so, and
would be angry at any delay.

" Then I will tell Gaston to hurry it on," he had said
evenly, and left the room to find Gaston.

Dinner went off better than Julia expected. As though
Paul sensed that she had not made up her mind about helping him the next evening, he tried to influence her gently by
setting himself to amuse her. He even recounted his efforts
to do business with a Japanese who could speak neither
French nor English, and whose interpreter had fallen suddenly ill. The effect had been laughable on both sides, for
each was convulsed with merriment at the pantomime act-
ing of the other.

At first Julia could see nothing to laugh at, but presently she thawed and allowed herself to smile.

" That is better," Paul encouraged. " You should laugh
more often, Miss Brown. You take life far too seriously."

That he should say such a thing to her! Did he not know
that whenever he chose to laugh she had been ready to echo
that laugh?

Now laughter crept into her voice and she retorted, " Perhaps I find so little in life to laugh at, monsieur."

" That is not possible. You with the world at your feet
are crazy to talk like that."

" The world! Is that where you think the world is? I
would never have thought of that. Well, one day I may be
curious enough to find out and do a grand round tour on
my savings. I promise you that once I start there will be
no catching up with me."

" We shall see about that," he remarked darkly.

She said confidently, enjoying teasing him, for as she
spoke his smile had faded, " What could you do to stop
me?"

" The question has not arisen, but if ever your dream

became a reality I expect I could move much faster than you."

But he looked at her as though he were puzzled, and presently when Gaston had served the coffee, and at a signal from Paul had left the room closing the door after him, Paul asked bluntly. " What is on your mind?"

She sighed. " So much! "

" Would you care to share it with me?"

" Oh, no, it is entirely personal." He was summarily shut out.

Then he asked, " What have you been doing today, apart from my business?"

" Thinking mostly," she confessed.

" About my simple request?"

" It isn't so simple to me. It looms a huge problem in my mind."

" Cut it out. Do as I want. You will never regret it, Miss Brown."

He was agitated, for he rose from the table, and unable to keep still, began to pace the room. Then abruptly he stopped close beside her and spread out his hands.

" I could understand your attitude if I had asked you to do something really big or unpleasant. This is merely granting a small favour, and you choose to imagine it a big thing and refuse to co-operate. What *is* the matter with you these days?"

Julia was silent. Said in these words he was making her behaviour seem churlish and disobliging.

It was then that Julia realised she would have to fall in with Paul's wishes. She thought angrily, Why do I hold back? But she knew. There was that faint thread of hope which she clung to. She thought, too, Even if I agree I write finis myself.

Something snapped within her.

Suddenly she wearied of the whole thing. The fight was too strong for her. She simply could not go on.

Quickly she decided to fall in with Paul's wishes, do

everything he wanted, and clear out. The sooner the better.

Suddenly, too, she cared no longer what happened to her. Julia's one wish now was to get away quickly.

Recklessly she pushed back her chair, her hands resting on the edge of the table. Tilting back her head her brown eyes met his rebelliously. At the same time she cried, " All right, I will, though I know you do not realise what you are asking me to do. I will dress up for your guests, put on a super show, act as I have never acted before, but I shall never give you the chance of asking me such a favour again. I owe you nothing. Our friendship, if you like to call it that, is ended."

Paul leant over her, his arms outstretched, his fingers clasping her wrists like steel.

" Now what do you mean by that?" he demanded savagely.

" What I say, Monsieur Roth. You can take a month's notice. I cannot remain in your employment."

There was a pause of consternation on both sides. This bombshell was unexpected. Then Paul cried, " Our contract says *three* months, Miss Brown." He was breathing heavily.

" All right, three," she amended passionately. " Let go of my wrists please. You hurt."

Paul let her go at once and straightened his back " I am sorry, but you drove me to it." He tried to speak formally but failed. He seemed very upset. She saw that he was trembling.

She rose to her feet rubbing her wrists which were red. " I will say good night, monsieur," she said unevenly. " If you have any instructions about tomorrow evening please leave them with Gaston."

" I have none. You know what to do. The only thing which I was about to say is that you can take the whole day off to prepare for the evening."

" Thank you." Her lips were stiff.

Paul turned his back on her. Even before she left the salon he was already in his room with the door shut.

Chapter Thirteen

THE FOLLOWING day was interminable to Julia, but slowly
it passed into evening. During the night she had faced the
position with Paul, and her mind was hardened against him.
She had failed with him. He had treated her badly. It was
now up to her to end this torture of mind which living in
his apartment and seeing him constantly had imposed upon
her. There was going to be no three months' notice. If Paul
chose to sue her for breach of contract he must do so, but
nothing would stop her leaving France tomorrow. That if
he knew he might try to prevent her going she felt sure,
which left her no alternative but to run away, as Chantal
had done, probably because there was no other way of
cutting loose. Julia, her mind cold and clear, her will in-
flexible, her actions deliberate, went to an Air Company

and booked herself a seat on the eight o'clock plane leaving Orly for London in the morning. That done she went around the corner from the apartment to an automobile company often engaged by Paul, and booked an auto to take her to Orly. The car was to be outside the apartment block at seven o'clock, to give her time to go through the customs and be ready to board the plane twenty-five minutes before it took off. As with Paul the chauffeur was told to wait quietly outside and not disturb the other residents.

Then Julia visited the hairdresser. She had her hair restyled in a sophisticated way, which even if no one liked, gave her confidence.

Returning to the apartment, still in that detached, cold manner which seemed part of her today, she took out the gold lamé evening dress from its black tissue paper covering, and which she had never had occasion to wear, and put it on a hanger. Marie had told her it was a model, worn by one of the young princesses of France, then sold to a film star, and now it was a part of Julia's meagre wardrobe. The dress had been to a cleaner recommended by Marie. It glittered in the sunshine, and Julia knew it fitted like a sheath of gold in artificial light.

Gaston laid the table in the salon early. He was proud of his work and called Julia to see it. She praised it wholeheartedly. She had no criticism to offer. She had arranged the flowers, the mimosa and freesias in slender vases about the room. Their smell was heavy and cloying in the atmosphere. The roses Julia kept for the table. They matched the candles in the candelabra. The wines had been on the side table since morning, taking on the room temperature.

If Gaston, puzzled by her quietness, stopped occasionally to contemplate her serious expression, Julia did not know it, and though Gaston would have liked to see her smile he said nothing.

Her feelings still numb Julia retired to rest for the remainder of the afternoon.

Later, when it was dark, she heard the front door open and shut. With a pang of anguish Julia realised that Paul had arrived home earlier than usual. She waited, hand on her heart, for him to send Gaston to her with a message, but none came, and gradually the wild beating of her heart subsided. Indeed, there was no reason at all why he should speak to her. Surely even he could find no fault in the preparations?

So while she lay on her back in bed, resting under the eiderdown, her hair carefully netted to keep it undisturbed, she closed her eyes which were painful, trying not to think of anything, but it was impossible to keep her mind blank when Paul was so disturbingly near.

Later Marie spared a short while from her cooking to help Julia dress.

" Nevaire, 'ave I seen such a dress, so *ravissante*, so much perfection," she cried when Julia was dressed. She remarked that it was a pity Julia had no jewels, and even suggested that Monsieur might have some locked away in his safe which he would lend her for the occasion, but Julia refused to wear any jewellery.

" But I would like some brandy, Marie," she said. " Something to boost my courage at the beginning of this important evening."

She was determined to play her part well.

Marie brought the brandy, and presently, wearing the gold lamé dress and with her head held high, Julia went into the salon.

Paul was already there, choosing some cigars from a small cedar-wood cabinet. Hearing her enter he turned his head sharply, then exclaimed and spun round to face her.

" Mees Brown! " His voice was breathless. " It is you! " He went over to her, his eyes alight with homage—or could it be worship for this girl? " You are so different. Your hair! This dress! "

The brown eyes met his coolly. " Do you like it? I am so

glad." She spoke with an artificial lightness which did not deceive him at all.

He took her hand and bending low carried it to his lips.

Julia sighed, and that sigh moved Paul strangely. It brought her closer to him and he was glad, for since last night he had felt cut off from her, out in the wilderness, more miserable than he had been for months, but now he felt that even if slight there was still a bond between them.

She withdrew her hand quickly. She glanced at the table, gleaming with silver and crystal, and around the room at the lovely flowers overloading the atmosphere with their perfume. "How do you like everything?" she asked, flinging her arm out in a sweeping, graceful gesture.

"It is magnificent. It could not be better. I am indeed grateful to you, and lucky in that I have found someone to please me so entirely. It is like having a second self come to life."

"Will your guests be late?"

He shrugged. "How can I tell? As I remember, Chantal was never punctual, I do not see how she could change."

"Yet you dislike unpunctuality in others," Julia heard herself saying.

The inference was that Chantal though unpunctual was never blamed.

"One forgives a lovely woman so much."

"So I suppose." She spoke coldly, and Paul wished he had not made the remark. He tried to make amends.

"Just as I would forgive *you* anything tonight," he complimented.

To his astonishment she laughed. "But I do not want your forgiveness for anything, monsieur. And if I did I should not care to plead for something I do not value."

That was a nasty one, but he only retorted mildly, "I was merely pointing out that there is more than one lovely woman in the world."

"Of course—many." And then she said in cold measured tones that fell so strangely from her soft lips and which he

hated, " This evening you will understand that I am playing a part for the sake of your guests. I may do and say
things which you could construe into real friendship, but
they mean nothing at all. I have no friendly feelings towards
you."

His face darkened. She was treating him like a complete
stranger, and that was the last thing he wanted between
them.

He retorted, " You are doing your best to spoil my evening."

" Oh no. I should not do that."

" I have told you I will explain everything satisfactorily
tomorrow. Please wait."

" Tomorrow! " She sat down suddenly, saying in a gay
mood, " I had some brandy in my bedroom, but the warm
effect has worn off. Please mix me a drink. We can always
have more when your guests arrive."

" Our guests," he corrected half-angrily.

Julia shrugged as though to say it was all the same to her.
Paul had an odd feeling that he was not forgiven for foisting
his guests upon her, and that nothing would ever be quite
the same between them again.

Meanwhile he mixed the drinks and watched her covertly,
not only because he enjoyed looking at her, but because she
was so brilliant and strange, even hard, and fascinated him
if only because he could not understand her.

When he handed her the glass she took it without looking
at him, saying, " Thank you," in an absent-minded way,
obviously not giving him her attention.

Then the bell rang and within moments Chantal in a
soft pink dress, and her husband were announced.

As in a dream Julia watched Paul and Chantal meet,
heard the swift interchange of short sentences of two people
who have long been parted meeting again in an atmosphere
of excitement, talk between Chantal and Paul that was so
smart it left her laughing, without attempting to understand
one word of it.

In a slow tempo she heard Chantal pause for breath, then say,

"You remember my husband, Paul?"

"Oh very well." There was a short laugh and Paul said, "We were business associates before he ever knew of your existence." Paul looked at Julia. "This is Chantal, Miss Brown," he said simply, and the two girls shook hands, appraising each other swiftly, each admitting silently that the other was beautiful.

Chantal giggled, "Is it always Miss Brown?" she inquired archly.

"It began that way, and it goes on," Paul replied shortly.

"But you and I—" she began, when Paul interrupted blandly.

"We were different."

Julia heard the odd intonation in his voice, and she thought swiftly, Everything was different for you two. All the world was Eden then. I believe it is now. Aloud she said coolly, softly, and yes, charmingly, "But of course it was different, you were such friends. What could one expect? Monsieur and I have been boss and secretary—"

Paul found himself listening to Julia's well-modulated voice. How different she was tonight. It was not only the dress and hair-style, the change was in Julia herself.

She said to Chantal, "I have heard so much about you—"

"Not from Paul?" Chantal said in surprise.

"No, we have never discussed his lady friends. That would be indiscreet. I heard it from others who knew you both."

She took no notice of Paul whose eyebrows were raised pointedly.

"Oh, do tell me," Chantal begged prettily.

"I couldn't. I forget anyway. I have not a good memory for some things."

"You can't stop people talking."

" No, you can't."

" By the time a tale gets round it has little semblance to
the truth," Chantal sighed.

" I am sure it hasn't."

" Anyway, I've been in Paul's bad books for so long now,
have I not Paul?"

He handed her a drink. " Indeed you have," he said
calmly.

Julia smiled. " But she is looking so lovely tonight in
her pink Dior dress that you must have forgiven her, as you
said just now you forgive all lovely women everything."

Paul paused then he grinned. He retorted, " For what it
is worth I forgave Chantal long ago." He looked at Chantal.
" As for your Dior dress, even without you in it I adore it.
Never have I seen such a magnificent creation. Did you
wear it to enchant me?"

Chantal's husband looked pleased.

Julia felt like saying, " She wore it to impress *me*, well
aware that she would succeed." And instantly she felt her
own dress garish and in bad taste, and her confidence fell
to a low ebb, and she thought despairingly, What inferior
weapons I have to fight with! But making an effort she
managed to say, " She has certainly done so, monsieur."

Then Chantal's husband asked Julia, " How long have
you been in Paris?"

" Soon after you and Chantal were married."

" That was a long while ago."

" In point of time, a matter of months."

He was merely trying to be friendly, but to Julia in her
present mood he seemed to cross-question her like a Q.C.
at a trial.

" You speak French well."

All Frenchmen say that, she thought, he probably thinks
I speak vilely.

" Thank you."

" Do you like it here?"

" No; I am not staying."

" Indeed, do you not like Paris? It is so gay."

" Paris is enchanting, but I have not seen much of it. And naturally the people one meets make a difference to one's outlook."

" But of course. We are here for such a short while, or I am sure we could remedy that."

" I am sure you would."

" When we pass through on our return journey—"

" I shall be back in London."

" Do not be in a hurry to leave us." As if it mattered whether she did or not!

" A secretary has little spare time for sightseeing."

Chantal overheard the remark. " You should not permit Paul to keep your nose to the grindstone," she said. " In my day—"

Julia rubbed the tip of her nose gently in a rueful gesture and they all laughed. " Things were different then. Perhaps Monsieur learnt a trick or two from you, which he practised on the new secretary who happened to be me."

" Not one or two, Miss Brown, but many," Paul corrected gently. " Perhaps I overdid the caution."

No one asked what he meant by that.

They had a couple of cocktails each, then Gaston served dinner which began with a rich *pâte de fois gras* from Strasbourg served with bits of crisp toast.

Chantal sat on the opposite side of the table to her husband. She said to Julia, " Last time I dined here I sat in your place."

" You were Monsieur's hostess?"

" Oh yes, always that."

" And now you are his guest, so much less exacting, don't you think?"

" I liked being Paul's hostess," protested Chantal.

Julia laughed. She glanced at Paul, her brown eyes mischievous and mocking, " ' Oh memories that bless and burn '! " she quoted.

Only Paul understood the allusion. He said lightly, " They

might, only I have few memories of that description."

Julia looked prettily puzzled. "But I quite thought—" she hesitated, then shrugged her shoulders.

Paul warned, "Before long you are going to find that most of your thoughts about me are wrong."

"Really?"

"How simple life could be if women would not insist on weaving complications into it." And now he looked at Chantal not Julia.

Not to be outdone by his wife's deliberate renewal of what he suspected had been a mad flirtation with Paul, Chantal's husband turned deliberately to Julia. He praised her dress extravagantly. He discussed the next course at dinner with the knowledge of a gourmet. He praised the wine.

Julia said truthfully if a little sadly, "I did not choose this dinner. I do know something of food, but nothing of wines, monsieur. Marie is a wonderful chef. I should not dare to pit my knowledge against hers."

"This *filet mignon* for instance. What would you . . ." and Chantal's husband talked about cooking far more expertly than Paul had ever done.

Julia discovered that Chantal drank too much. She also chattered too much, and was inclined to be indiscreet with Paul in a way that she, Julia, would never have dared to be. Her big eyes were dewy and brilliant, and often dwelt affectionately on Paul. Once she put her hand over his which was resting on the tablecloth. He looked at it, but did not move, though when, presently Chantal released it he picked up his glass and drank some more of his own special burgundy which he had chosen to go with the streak.

Paul looked at Julia. It was the only time he had addressed her directly since the meal began. "I know you do not care for burgundy, so I have brought out a special claret for you," he said.

She flushed at the attention. "You should not have done that, monsieur."

" Why not? You find the burgundy too heavy. Everyone must have what he likes."

There was a delicious sweet made of chestnut cream, ratafia and Madeira wine which Julia was able to announce had been made specially for her by Marie.

" She never concocted a sweet for me," Chantal complained. Her cheeks were flushed and she looked like a pretty spoilt child, with her hair a little tousled and her eyes shining like stars.

" Perhaps you never showed any interest in her cooking," said Julia.

" I do not pretend to like it. Why should I when I have no intention of cooking?" pouted Chantal, but she looked so lovely in her pink dress that the fact whether she would make a good housewife or not did not seem to matter.

Paul listened, but he said nothing.

Suddenly it came to Julia that her own dress was wrong. Her hair-do was wrong. Everything about her was too sophisticated, and she was not old enough to carry it off. She should have been content with the dress she had brought from London. It was good and unpretentious. The colour suited her. She was certainly more at home with her usual hair-do than with this upswept coiffure which gave her command of a situation she could not take.

Chantal's dress was lovely. It was suitable to her age. It enhanced her perfect skin. It was young and gay.

And with that knowledge, that her armoury was at fault, Julia flopped. In spite of her frantic efforts to pretend a gaiety she did not feel she knew that the party was quickly " going dead " on her.

She looked at Chantal's glowing face for inspiration, then despairingly her eyes sought Paul's.

To her astonishment he was looking at her, his expression inscrutable.

She had no idea of what he was thinking. Silently she appealed to him for help. Julia never knew it but Paul's eyes had been riveted on her face for some moments, and he had seen what had disturbed him deeply, the saddest expression he had ever surprised in a human face. But with a lover's intuition he observed that Julia's expression was changed, and that Julia was asking him to help in some way.

Without pausing he said the first words that came into his head. " Shall we dance before coffee or after?"

Chantal's husband looked shocked, but neither of the girls thought the remark unusual. Chantal jumped to her feet, rocked unsteadily, then went forward into Paul's arms.

He said, " A moment! We cannot dance without music. I have a transistor in my bedroom. I will get it."

Chantal followed him into the bedroom. While she waited for them to reappear Julia chatted lightly to Chantal's husband. She was not conscious of what she said, only that she had to make conversation to keep him from chasing after his wife.

Presently they were dancing to the thin sound of the transistor, and a little later, when Chantal tripped over a mat, Paul put her into a chair saying, " You sit down and steady yourself while I dance with Julia."

This was the first time Paul had held her in his arms, and Julia trembled at his touch, and wondered how she could endure his hold without some of the ecstasy that thrilled her communicating itself to him. This was heaven, or was it? Unfortunately Julia's dress allowed very little leg room, and the dance together was a failure.

As I might have guessed, a mortified Julia admitted to herself, when she had trodden on Paul's toes several times.

" You are out of practice," shouted Chantal, who though dancing with her husband, kept a keen eye on Paul and Julia.

" Not at all. It is the tight dress," Paul replied. He stopped then and said laughingly to Julia, " You cannot be fashionable *and* a good dancer."

" I did not expect to dance. I'm sorry," she said in a low voice.

" Let us go on," he urged gallantly.

But Chantal was laughing merrily, and Julia shook her head. She managed to smile with Chantal. " I am supposed to be a good dancer," she told her defiantly.

" Not in that dress, *chérie*."

" The dress has failed me."

Neither of the men would agree to this.

At midnight the guests went home, and Paul said he would take them down in the lift and see them safely off the premises. " We do not have a night porter. Once a guest went down in the lift and got stuck halfway. He remained there until the morning, when they found him asleep in a corner."

Everyone thought this a good joke.

When Paul returned to the apartment he found the salon empty. Julia had gone to her room.

He thought of asking her to return to the salon and having another drink with him. He might even have found an opportunity to beg for her friendship, but he had so much to explain to her that he decided against it. Julia was tired. She had seemed to him dispirited. Paul could not forget that strange haunted look he had surprised in her eyes, though what it meant he did not know.

Let her be, he thought sympathetically, pouring out a stiff brandy for himself.

Chapter Fourteen

ONCE LOCKED in her room Julia took off the gold lamé dress and flung it over a chair. Her love for it had waned. Earlier in the evening she had believed Marie's fulsome compliments, but not now. She had thought Monsieur liked the dress. Now she knew he was only like all other Frenchmen, full of compliments about clothes, perhaps to pretend they were clothes-minded. She kicked off her shoes, then tore off the false toupée pinned to her own back-combed hair which the hairdresser had used and commingled in an artful hair-do, with so much care. She threw it on the dressing-table, combed out her own hair—and felt better.

The evening for her had been an increasing mountain of despair, an unequal fight against Chantal who held all the cards and who knew instinctively how to play them. It was clear to Julia from many little feminine pointers that Chantal had ruled over Paul and his household with an iron hand. She still reigned like a queen in the salon. She had the Frenchwoman's art of pleasing a man and putting it to good use for herself. And why not? One could not blame Chantal for taking care of No. 1. Then Chantal had evidently acquired more taste in clothes than she, Julia, had. She had far more money to spend on them, an adoring husband to pet her, and a still doting lover to keep her young. What Julia could not hope to guess was why Paul had asked Chantal to dine here this evening, unless it was to show up his new secretary's weaknesses, and to humiliate her further.

Well, all that was over. There would be no more fighting or stormy passages between Paul and herself. He would not have the chance of humiliating her further. All was at an end between them, if indeed there had been any beginning.

Quietly Julia packed her clothes, until the case would hold no more, leaving some over for the little case which she would send for later. She put out the tweed dress and fur-collared coat she would be travelling in tomorrow, and filled her handbag with trifles she might want on the journey. She must leave the apartment at seven o'clock. She would be in the plane heading for London by the time Gaston brought in her *petit-déjeuner*, and discovered that she had gone. Julia's one worry was whether she would oversleep at six o'clock and not be downstairs at seven. But there was too much at stake for her to do that.

All her movements were quiet and deliberate. She prepared as in a dream. She had no regrets about leaving her room which though small was most comfortable. Indeed Julia took pains to assure herself that she was free to go, and that she was only using her freedom. She meant to cut Paul out of her life. It did not bear thinking about, but when she was away from France, with no chance of meeting him or hearing his voice, she could face up to anything, even the loss of Paul, whose mind had always been filled with Chantal's image he could see no other woman.

Julia did not cry. She did not want to cry. Tears would come later but she dared not waste time now in crying.

At last, when all was ready, and the room tidy, Julia undressed and got into bed. She fell asleep quickly and did not wake until five o'clock. She rose soon afterwards afraid that if she remained in bed she would fall asleep, and oversleep.

At seven Julia crept out of the apartment, lugging her heavy suitcase, and hurried as quickly as possible downstairs, round and round until she reached the ground floor. She had to stand on her suitcase to pull down the bolt of the door. The air in the street was cold and keen.

A long black sleek auto, like a beetle waited at the kerb for her.

The chauffeur took her case and she got in saying, "Have I kept you waiting?"

"No, m'm'selle. I have been here but five minutes."

"How long will it take to get to Orly?"

"Not more than half an hour."

But it did. When the car should have reached Orly, it was only halfway there, having broken down. By the time the chauffeur had found an early taxi and Julia was rushed to the airport, it was nearly eight o'clock.

By this time she was worried. She was hurried through the customs, then halted in the departure lounge. "You are too late for the eight o'clock plane, m'm'selle. See, she is out there, taxi-ing on to the runway."

"But I must catch it."

The porter shrugged.

"She is only waiting. Surely I can board her?"

"No one is allowed out there. It is dangerous. You can take the next one."

"When is that?"

"In an hour's time."

"An hour. I can't wait that long."

The porter spoke to someone higher-up, and so on until Julia was interviewed by a senior official, who told her,

" The plane has gone. Better wait in the departure lounge, or have some *déjeuner* in the café. Time soon passes. I am sorry m'm'selle, but the rules are that passengers must arrive twenty-five minutes before the plane is scheduled to take off. If you had come fifteen minutes before the hour I would have done my best to get you off by that plane, but you left it too late.

Julia bit her lips. She went into the café and had some coffee, then restlessly she went back to the departure lounge and sat unobtrusively in a corner looking at a newspaper. It had occurred to her that Paul might follow her, but she had not accepted the thought seriously. Paul would be only too glad to get rid of her. It was not a nice thought, but she had to face the fact, even though it left her more troubled and frightened than ever before.

Over the top of the paper she saw that people were beginning to queue up for the next plane. She must join them in a few moments.

Someone touched her shoulder sharply. She jumped, and was still. Then a voice repressed with fury and fear, trying hard to speak quietly, said, " So here you are! I would never have thought you could behave so badly to me. How dare you run away from me like a common cheat and coward. You will come back with me at once. I want to talk to you."

She turned suddenly and looked up into the face of a man she had never seen before, a changed Paul with a grey lined face and staring eyes, and yes—an unshaven jaw.

She shook off his hand. " But I don't want to talk to you. Through a mishap I have lost the eight o'clock plane, but I shall leave on the nine o'clock."

" You are not going by that either. If you wanted to leave me there was nothing to stop you, but you could have gone decently at mid-day or during the afternoon. You can still go then if you want, but only after we have had our talk."

" What talk? We have talked for months. I am sick of talking to you. It gets us nowhere."

He saw by her manner that she did not mean to go with him, that she was unwilling to return to the apartment, and he dared not risk a scene for then that really might be the end. He knew, too, that whatever happened he must not make a mess of everything. He must try to pull off a bluff.

He asked, " Why are you running away to London?"

" That is not your business."

" Oddly, everything concerning you is my business."

She laughed scornfully, but there was no mirth in the laugh.

" So! What are you going to do about it?"

" I will tell you. It is so much my business that if you do not come with me at once without further argument, I mean to create a scene in this public place, and I know who will come off the worse."

That stirred her. " You wouldn't dare!" But clearly from the hunted way she glanced about her she was frightened. " This is terrible! It is blackmail!"

" I would dare anything to get you back. Come, people are staring at us. There is not time to waste, especially if you mean to return here later in the day."

" Do you think I *want* to hurry back to London?" she cried furiously.

" Then why go?"

" Because there is nothing for me now in Paris."

" Who said so?"

" I do."

" You are wrong."

" I am right."

They glared venomously at each other. Then Paul picked up her case. " Is this yours? Have you been carrying this weight around? Come with me." He spoke sharply, his mind as jerky as his sentences. With his free hand he clutched her elbow tightly. He was taking no risk of a second escape.

They went out of the hall side by side, and Paul led her to the first taxi. He opened the door and propelled her in.

He gave the address of his apartment to the chauffeur and followed her in. He was still angry, his movements rough and abrupt.

She said tersely, " I suppose Gaston told you I had gone?"

" Yes, and within five minutes I was dressed and the hunt for you was on. I chose Orly. Gaston has gone to Le Bourget, and Marie to the Gare du Nord. One of us at least hoped to find you."

They did not see the janitor at the apartment building. From the clatter they guessed that he was emptying rubbish bins in the area below the pavement. Quietly they went up in the lift to the silent apartment where the morning's mail was still in the letter-box. The curtains had not been drawn in the salon and the lights still burned. Paul's *petit-déjeuner* tray was on the table. Gaston must have slapped it down before rushing to Monsieur's door with the bad news that Julia had flown. Some of the coffee was spilled.

Julia stood in the middle of the salon, not knowing what to do. She felt defeated and desolate. By now she should have been well on her journey, yet by an ill-stroke from fate she was still here, with everything about her muddled. And at the back of her mind was a dread that for some reason or other she might not be able to go at all. This thought unnerved her and she looked about wildly for a way of escape.

Paul had left the big case in the hall. He had followed her closely into the salon. Now, as he saw her eyes which were wide with fear, he quietly turned the key in the lock and leant against the door. Suddenly he was moved to action.

Stretching out his hand he swept off her little tweed cap, ruffling her hair. He unfastened her coat buttons because she made no effort to do so herself, then he took it off for her and pushed her into a big chair.

He switched off the lights and drew back the curtains, letting in the morning sunshine. The room was untidy, as it was left when the party ended last night. Ashtrays were full. There were dirty glasses, and cushions needed plumping up. Regardless of the mess, Paul lighted a cigarette. He flung himself into a chair facing Julia and contemplated her in heavy silence before he spoke. "Will you have your *petit-déjeuner* now or wait until we have had our talk?"

"Let's get this talk over first."

"*Bien.*" Then he said. "I am beside myself with anger. That you of all people could stoop so low as to creep out of my apartment like a thief in the night, while I slept! You have gone down in my esteem. What on earth can you say to explain such behaviour?" He felt calmer now that she was safe again under his roof.

Julia shrugged. "Nothing, only that Chantal got away with it," she remarked resentfully.

So she knew all about that business. Paul's face was convulsed. "Forget her. I had no idea you wanted to imitate her bad example."

"She succeeded where I failed."

Paul explained acidly, "Chantal succeeded because when it was discovered she had left the apartment, I made no immediate attempt to look for her. I let her go because even before she went I had decided that she would never make me happy, and that it was best for us to part. I was only awaiting a chance to tell her so. I recall the morning she went quite clearly. I rose as usual, bathed and shaved and ate my *petit-déjeuner* by my open window. Afterwards I made inquiries. The police found Chantal for me. I know you have heard some queer tales about my undying love for her. But I was never in love with Chantal. I admired her loveliness as I would a picture. What I suffered from was infatuation. I was an envied man basking in her aura. But you are a different proposition, as I soon learned after you came to live in this apartment."

"I know," Julia cried passionately, her voice contrasting with his even, almost colourless tones. "You have never let me forget it. I am inferior in every way to the perfect

Chantal." Her lips trembled. She tried to keep her end up before those watching eyes. But coming back here so unexpectedly, and being close to him in this room, was proving too great a strain for her. She turned her head away sharply, so that he should not see her eyes were full of tears.

So Julia did not see Paul's eyes widen with amazement at her accusation that he thought her inferior to Chantal.

"Inferior! Ridiculous! I have never used that word when comparing you with Chantal. I have certainly never thought of her as approaching perfection. I do not care for such people. They are usually so inhuman."

"You may not have used words to express your thoughts, but nevertheless you have inferred it. Look at her dress last night. You knew that her husband is rich and can buy anything Chantal wants. You knew she would naturally put on a good show against me. All you warned me to wear was my prettiest dress. Well, I wore my only one, and what a sight I looked. Neither the dress nor the hair style suited me."

"Because they gave you a sophistication you have not got. The time to wear a dress like that is when you are forty." Then he went on impatiently, "But all this is trivial and beside the point. It did not worry me at all. You were not humiliated in any way last night, as you seem to think. Besides, I had promised that you should not be. Have you no faith in me? If you know so much perhaps you will tell me why I asked Chantal and her husband to dinner last night? It could not to be relive old memories for there are none."

But Julia only shook her head. She could not answer.

"Then I will tell you. I wanted to be quite satisfied in my own mind that my infatuation for Chantal's charm was over before I told you what was growing in my heart for you. I needed to see you together. It took me less than five minutes to decide. You see, I know the kind of girl you are, or I thought I did until this morning, though now I do not know what to think. I am as puzzled as you are at the way things have turned out."

He was clearly perplexed. He loved this girl. He was choked by emotion. Nothing she did or said would change his deep love. But what were her feelings for him? Yesterday he would have thought she liked him, not as he did her, but he would teach her to love him soon, as the path before them was reasonably clear. Yet now that she had run away from his house, he felt sure of nothing. He was even frightened in case Julia told him that she was running away from *him*. That would be catastrophic news.

So he cried abruptly, " And now please no more talk of Chantal. We have already wasted far too much of our precious time on her. I want to talk about us."

He scolded Julia for behaving so cruelly and thoughtlessly and running away so secretly. In spite of his fear of saying too much he managed to talk himself into a better humour.

Meanwhile with a rush of emotion it came to Julia that perhaps she had been in too great a hurry to play her cards recklessly. She had done something Paul would not find it easy to forgive. She tried to carry off this new disappointment with a high hand, and wished that when he offered her some *petit-déjeuner* she had accepted. Over the coffee a better spirit might have been created. Surely Paul could guess that she was sorry for causing him to worry, not forgetting Gaston and Marie, neither of whom had returned? What a fool she had made of herself!

It seemed as though her whole life had toppled about her in ruins, and she was aghast with the mess she had made of everything.

Her voice was thick with tears that she could not hide as she cried, " It doesn't matter about anything any more. All these explanations have come too late. How was I to know what was in your mind? You never gave me a hint of what you thought. You stuck strictly to business."

" I think it does matter. Clearly it is your fault that any explanations have to be made at all. It all hitches on this running away. Do you not care a little what I think about

you? Of course I stuck to business, but I wanted to make
love to you, when you would have been frightened."

"Oh, leave me alone. You have said too much. I tell you
it is too late. Don't you understand that I wanted to hide
from you? If it makes you any happier then I am hurt, too."
And Julia thought, He must know I am a fool. I've said
and done all the wrong things. I must be mad.

"I am sorry. I suppose I should leave you alone, perhaps
help you on your way back to London. I will try to do so
if it will make you happy, but—God help me, I cannot. I
do not want you to go. I wish you to stay. I have never
wanted anyone so much."

A look of anguish crossed her face. She had lost love. She
bit her lips, trying to stop their trembling. In great distress
he saw tears roll down her cheeks and splash on her
shoulder. She could hide her grief no longer. It had taken
possession of her.

Then suddenly she collapsed. Her head bent and her out-
spread hands went up to cover her face. "Oh, dear, what
shall I do?" she wept, rocking a little to and fro in anguish.

Paul saw her shoulders heave spasmodically. She began
to cry in luxurious abandon, long heartrending sobs that
came from the depth of her being.

At first Paul, though he was deeply moved, made no effort
to stem this grief, thinking it must soon expend itself. But
the sobs increased, until he could stand the sound no longer.

He rose and went over to her, touching her shoulder
tentatively, "Don't cry," he said gently. "You will make
yourself ill if you go on like this much longer."

Words seemed to have no effect.

Paul's anger against her melted. She seemed so lonely
and lost, so much in need of love and care. What did it
matter what she had done or how she had treated him? He
loved her. He wanted only her love. If only she would not
repulse him! If only she would show her need of him, or
give him one word of hope!

"Julia!"

No answer.

Paul knelt beside the chair and put his arms around her, gathering her close to him, pressing her cheek to his breast, murmuring soft words of comfort.

" *Doucement*! *Doucement*! I hate that you should be so unhappy! "

Her handkerchief was wet and useless, and Paul took it from her. He pulled his own handkerchief from his pocket and wiped her eyes. " Use this," he said . . . That is better. I cannot bear that you should cry."

" I—am such a failure—"

" That is a word I never use."

" It is true. You know I am."

Paul smiled. " It is I who should cry. You ran out on me because you hated me so much."

She half-raised her head, though her voice was still thick. " That was not the reason. I went away because—"

She did not finish, the sound was stifled because Paul was nearly suffocating her. He was saying, " Oh, Julia, my darrrling, *je t'adore ma p'tite*," until the soft caressing words that were meant to comfort grew wild, full of longing and desire and passion. Just saying them revealed Paul's hungry heart.

At last what he whispered seemed to be making some impression on Julia, for her sobbing grew quieter, and Paul had the feeling that she was listening to him. Presently she drew away from him and wiped her eyes, half-apologising for her tears. Paul helped her use the handkerchief. He put his forefinger under her chin, saying, " Now smile, Julia."

She smiled through her tears and he said, " That is better. I hear sounds outside. Gaston and Marie must have come back. I will tell them to make some fresh coffee. You will like a hot drink?"

When he returned he was smiling, and said, " They came back very miserable having of course, drawn blanks, but were reassured when they saw your case in the hall." He passed his hand over his chin. " What upsets them now is my unshaven face. I must shave before the coffee comes or Gaston will think this is the end of our world instead of the beginning." He glanced at the closed door. " You will not leave the apartment while I am shaving?"

" No," she smiled with more assurance.

" If you decide to go, you will be content to wait for the afternoon?" he pursued.

" I have decided, Paul." Her eyes met his shyly and lovingly.

His face lightened. He came and took her in his arms, straining her to him as though he would never let her go. " So have I," he whispered, bending his head to hers and kissing her warmly. Then with a cry of love and triumph his mouth met hers in their first long passionate kiss.